RUNAWAY HORSE!

Leon frantically yanked on the reins, but nothing could have halted the panicked horse's plunge as he barreled downward. One foreleg hooked in a fissure and then came free as his knees folded; momentum cartwheeled him up and over. Leon's thin scream was choked off as the horse's weight crashed down on him. The horse rolled away and came to his feet at the bottom and stood there, trembling.

Leon lay twisted and quiet on the sunlit rocks. A stream of rubble ran down the bank against his body. Silence. . . . One thing was certain, Leon Manigault was stone-dead. Nobody could have his head wrenched at such an angle to his body and still be alive.

Track The Man Down

T. V. Olsen

LEISURE BOOKS   NEW YORK CITY

A LEISURE BOOK®

March 1998

Published by special arrangement with
Golden West Literary Agency

Dorchester Publishing Co., Inc.
276 Fifth Avenue
New York, NY 10001

ISBN 0-8439-4369-6

TRACK THE
MAN DOWN

Chapter One

For most of two days, Big Torrey had faced the raw-colored scarps of bald mesas and the baking glitter of old *playas* that fingered between them. Coming northward now into a sudden jog of foothills that bent up green and shaggy to the south slopes of the San Toscos, he thought it was like climbing out of a barren Hades into a young Eden. By God, it was all of that. A milk-and-honey land for sure. The crowns of gentle hills were darkened by thick piñon and cedar that off-straggled into the short valleys between, these rolling yellow with sun-cured grass. And water? Water should be plenty and pure up here.

Halting his tall black, Big unslung his canteen from the cantle. "Yessir, Tarbaby, it's sure-hell one pretty piece of country." He took a swig of brackish water, swished it around his mouth, and spat it out. "We can scare up better drinking than this swill. 'Bout all a body can't find right here is a shot of prime skullbuster to ease his water down on.''

The mare stamped her white-stockinged foot. Sixteen hands high, she was built beautifully solid for a huge-size rider. Any movement made her muscles surge like quicksilver. A splash of white starred her muzzle; only the star and stocking broke the all-over black sheen of her coat, now dulled by a dusting of red grit. She was still hanging prime after days of desert travel. Big had no sure idea of her ancestry, but the cowhand he'd won her off in a memorable night of tall-stake stud at Duke's Casino in Gilman had judged that a high-bred dam had got caught wrongside of her oatbag by someone's Injun mustang. Seemed a likely guess. Wasn't often that a big grain-fed brute like Tarbaby could easily take to a rough forage of tornillo beans and even, when necessary, to a diet of cactus with the spines burned away.

Big Torrey tipped back his battered rawhide hat and studied the lay of the country some more. He made out a twisty cord of pale green on a lowland meadow off east: a willow-grown stream for certain. Good place for a desert-beat man to throw his hull a day or so and just rest. Make camp under a big shady old tree. Hunt him up some tender-eating game and maybe wet a line in that creek. Just loaf a spell. Wasn't in a goddamn hurry to get someplace, was he? Yessir, right here seemed the ticket.

Gigging Tarbaby down a grassy slope barred by the long shadows of late afternoon, Big cut toward the meandering line of distant willow. He hadn't gone a hundred yards when, coming up on a brushy rise, he saw a pale thread of smoke erupt from an aspen grove upstream. He promptly pulled up, slitting his eyes. Someone feeding a cookfire? Seemed so. The faint barking of a dog reached him now, and something else. Sheep, thought Big, wrinkling his broad nose. Just a faraway whiff of 'em was worse'n that perfume that Santhy Mae, the colored madam down at Gilman, used to wear. Even Santhy Mae wouldn't abide this godawful stink; she had her pride, ol' Santhy did, and was generally partial to good cowman's smells.

"She-yit," Big muttered without much bite. He didn't really mind a whole lot. Basically a keep-to-himself sort, he was also an easygoing cuss whose democratic spirit could unbend to just about any halfway congenial company now and then. Be plenty of room to camp anywhere upwind of the woollies. Good idea, though, to reconnoiter these folks from downwind right now, keeping that dog in mind. Simple caution dictated that a man fixing to set up a spell on a piece of country unknown to him should size up its inhabitants. Not knowing their temper, he'd as soon spot them first.

Big cut slowly northeast, keeping the wind in his face along with its obnoxious roll of sheepstink and the dog's barking and then, rising like a murmurous tide, the blatting of those goddamn woollies. The grove of aspen cut off his view of the flock, but he had the smoke in sight. Coming to the willow-screened glint of water that marked the creek's crooked prowl, Big followed it upstream, holding to the thick willow growth and scattered mottes of aspen along the bank. He considered leaving Tarbaby and going in on foot, but a sneaky approach might leave these folks on edge, even after he'd showed 'em he meant no harm. Best get off on the right foot. . . .

Soon he came in sight of the sheep. They were pocketed on a tree-flanked meadow east of the camp grove; a huge brown dog was racing about, worrying them into a tight flock. Then a man's voice called, "Tigre!," and the dog,

9

who looked big and ugly enough to take on tigers, trotted off into the grove. Big lifted his '73 Winchester from its scabbard and balanced it across his pommel as he moved on into the trees. Almost at once he came to a small clearing, where a canvas-hooped wagon stood. He didn't see anyone right off, but now the dog got wind of him and started a ruckus fit to raise the dead.

A young man came stepping around the wagon. Seeing Big, he stopped in his tracks. "Tigre," he said sharply. *"¡Silencio!"* He held an old needle gun in his strong, square hands; his black eyes were nervous and watchful.

"Howdy." Big gave an easy grin as he spoke, halting at a half-quarter turn so that the youth couldn't miss his own slack-held Winchester.

The sheepherder didn't answer right off. Not much over twenty, he was a well-built fellow, with a handsome olive-skinned face and a shock of curly black hair. He wore leather breeches and a sheephide poncho turned woolly side out over a faded calico shirt. Leather-rope sandals shod his bare feet. He gave Big a long study from head to foot, then upward and over again, as if not altogether sure he was seeing right.

Big, accustomed to this sort of wondering scrutiny, let him take his time. You couldn't reasonably expect a body of any color to take in a great tough-faced hulk of a black man all in one gulp. Standing six-five in his sock feet, Big was built bull-heavy to match, all of it hard, solid weight. His hair was cropped close and tight to his round skull, emphasizing his slightly bat-winged ears, one of which was shapeless with scar tissue. His broad face had been often called "ugly as sin," usually by white folks who hadn't seen many full-blood Negroes, particularly one of his height and heft. Big himself didn't reckon it was too bad a face, allowing for the scars of old brawls, a twice-broken nose, and mostly that chawed-up ear.

Finally the youth gave a polite and cautious nod. *"Buenas tardes, Señor Negro."*

Big gave a deep, rich-bass chuckle, shoving his Winchester back in its boot. "Hell, boy, I got a name. Buford Torrey of Texas, that's me. Mostly they call me 'Big.' Mind if I light down?"

"You are not from Lionclaw?"

"That big cow outfit I hear tell of in these parts? Nope. Drifting through."

"Ah." The youth's smile streaked white and sudden across his face, easing its strained look. "Señor Big, huh? That's a ver' good name. *¡Qué hombre!* My name, she's Luis Ayala. *Silencio*, El Tigre."

The dog stood braced and hackle-raised, his throaty growls deepening as Big swung out of his saddle. "Man, that's a fine whopper of a dog. Take a man's leg right off with them big jaws."

Luis nodded agreeably. "*Sí*, I think so. This, she's Meramee. Is my wife."

An Indian girl had come light-footing around the wagon, her eyes bright with curiosity. She stopped, clapping a hand over her mouth in surprise, when she saw Big. She was around seventeen, plump and brown, and a sightly creature for sure. Navajo she looked like, with her black wool skirt and blue velvet blouse, her silver bracelets and hair beads.

Big swept his hat off, kind of bowing. *"Buenas tardes, señora,"* he said in his best border Mex. "A thousand pardons if I startled you."

Luis laughed. "Maramee don' talk English or Spanish. We make the signs to talk. You eat with us, eh? You like mutton stew?"

11

"If that's what I smell cooking, you are on, sheep boy. Lemme hobble out my horse on this good grass and I be right with you."

"No, Señor Big, you are the guest. I take care of the horse. Sit and eat."

Grandly he motioned Big to the other side of the wagon, where a tripod-hung stewpot was bubbling over a low fire. "Meramee—" Luis touched his belly and lips, then gestured at Big. She smiled and nodded. It was a very neat, very clean camp, Big noted with an appreciative eye as he seated himself on the ground tailor-fashion and accepted the tin bowl of stew that Meramee ladled out for him.

Luis whistled and sang, laughed and talked, as he tied Tarbaby out by a couple of team horses on a patch of grass not far from the wagon. It tickled a man just to watch and listen to him, Big thought. He couldn't remember seeing anyone so bursting with the juices of life and reveling in every second of it. Yet he wondered about the boy's demeanor at first sight of him.

Lionclaw . . . he'd heard aplenty of that outfit.

Still rattling on, Luis sat down cross-legged by the fire; Meramee handed him a bowl of stew and filled one for herself. "She don' know my talk; I don' know hers," Luis grinned. "Yet we com'pren' ver' good, us. Is fonny, no?"

Big didn't think so. He could almost feel the perfect understanding between these two. Whatever their improvised sign language didn't communicate, their eyes did. Blamed good stew, he thought, spooning it up with the appetite of a man who'd been living for days on jerky and make-do of one sort or another. Seasoned kind of odd to his taste, though. He'd never savored anything of the like, not even in Mexico, and now he wondered what sort of Spanish breed this Luis Ayala was.

12

Luis' bright, curious glance took in Big's worn cow-man's gear and the faded thick-weave Saltillo *serape* he wore poncholike over his shabby range clothes. Big took the steaming cup that Meramee handed him. Though partly made of ground-up mesquite beans, the coffee was strong and savory. And he was delighted to find that it was mixed with chili juice.

"Man, that's prime." He smacked his lips. "Ain't no other way to drink it."

"Ha!" Luis was tossing bones to El Tigre, who caught and crunched them up like so many goober peas. "Now I *know* you live' in Mexico, señor."

"Sure thing. Spent ten year there." Big nodded appreciatively as Meramee took his bowl and cup away for re-fills. "My folks run away to Mexico in '55. I was just twelve."

"*¿Qué?* . . . run away?"

"Yeh. We was slaves. Near all us black people was, didn't you know that? Started in Georgia, my folks did. Our master, he come to Texas after the Mexican War, which he fit in. Got a headright league of land and set out to raise cattle. I got part raised on a ranch in the Panhandle. Palo Duro country, you'd maybe call it. There was hundreds of white ranchers in Texas had crews of slave nig-gers. And they was a few thousand of us who ran away to Mexico and stayed till the war was over. Me, I learned the cow trade from Mexico *vaqueros*. Ain't no better teach-ers." Big pitched into his second helpings. "But I lay odds you don't hail from Mexico."

"No, Señor Big. I am Basque from Navarra."

"Huh. That's a diff'rent one on me."

"We Basques, we ver' diff'rent people. Some live in Spain, some in France. But every place diff'rent from other

13

people. We got diff'rent language, diff'rent ways. We like to dance, to sing, and we are ver' honest, but we are good smugglers.'' Luis laughed. ''Say, you like to hear song?''

''Sure,'' Big grinned. ''Sing it sweet, sheep boy.''

''Wait.'' Luis got up and walked to the tailgate of his wagon, and rummaged inside. He came back to the fire bearing a guitar and a leather wine bag.

Big chuckled. ''Boy, you making music already.''

Luis handed him the wine bag and sat down again, lightly picking at the guitar strings. Big, not daunted by a full belly, opened the mouth of the wine bag and raised it high and tipped it and then, squeezing hard, threw his head back and sent a flat stream into his open mouth. His Adam's apple bobbed for a long time. When he lowered the skin bag, Luis was gazing at him in awe. ''Santa Maria,'' he murmured.

The golden-sweet explosion of sour wine ran like hot honey through Big's veins. Luis drank with an expertise that matched Big's. Laying the wine bag aside then, he launched into a wild song full of strange notes and unfamiliar cadences. Big had never heard the like, but now, as he began to pick up the rhythm, he clapped his big hands in time to it. Meramee joined in, and pretty soon the late afternoon was alive with their laughter and shouting. Big leaped to his feet and began kicking up his heels in an improvised dance that was somewhere between Africa and hoedown country.

When Luis finally closed on a rippling chord, Big flung himself, exhausted and laughing, to the ground. ''Boy, you do know how to make that twang box do tricks!'' He cooled his tonsils with another shot of wine. Why hell, this was about as heady and pluperfect enjoyable an occasion

14

as he'd ever known; Big felt a powerful welling warmth toward his hosts.

"Basques, by God, some people you must be!"

Luis smiled, stroking his fingers across the strings. "Don' your people sing, señor?"

"Sure they do, boy. Just they mix in a heap of tears."

Strumming lightly, Luis began to talk in a soft, fine voice of his native land and its small farms with their sloping meadows and hand-fed cows in stable, its apple orchards and high sheep pastures. Of his father, condemned to poverty by a traditional law of inheritance that gave all his family's property to a single brother. Whereupon his father had journeyed to America, to California. But the little valley farm he'd bought was suddenly ruined by rivers of mud washed down from a hydraulic mining operation on the mountainflank above, ruination that had broken the elder Ayala's heart; he had died shortly after. Luis had vowed never to own land and, keeping that vow, had always drifted as the mood stirred him, owning so little that it would excite envy in nobody. Now, of course, he had Meramee, having given her Navajo father twenty sheep, then taking her to the mission at San Catalina to be baptized that they might be married in the Holy Church.

"Are you of the faith, Señor Big?"

"Well, not 'xactly that one, boy. 'Bout the only way my folks didn't go Mex was, they stayed Baptist. Most of all of us did. But we got treated a heap better below the border than ever we was above it."

Luis' teeth gleamed. "Ah . . . is a good life we got. There is freedom, eh? Is sun and stars, grass and trees. But best is to be free. Free as wind. You feel so too, eh?"

"Says about all a man got to know," Big agreed, grinning, and raised the wine bag again. The goodness of this

15

time, this hour, held him like a pool of warm molasses. He wanted to stretch it for memory's sake, for there weren't many hours in a man's whole life that tended to jell just so. . . .

The dog raised his head, rumbling growls. A ridge of hair bristled up along his spine. What the hell, Big thought. He glanced about, but nothing seemed amiss. Without a word, Luis got up and moved toward his rifle leaning on the wagon tongue.

"You all hold still like you are," a voice said. "Keep your hand offen that piece, spick, or I blow your goddamn head off."

Luis had halted by his rifle, but his hand stopped inches short of the weapon. Brush rustled faintly at Big's back. Slowly, his spine crawling, he lowered the wine bag. He turned his head till the tail of his eyes framed the gleam of a gun barrel sticking out of the foliage. A thick gold glow of sunset filled the glade, and in the dead silence you could have heard a pine needle drop.

Whoever it was holding the rifle, he was a crafty-quiet one. Had stolen up without a sound on the only side of the camp that was flanked by thick brush.

"*Santa Maria . . . !*" A chagrined, explosive whisper escaped Luis.

Again brush stirred; the man stepped out to view. He moved with a rangy-tall grace; a ruff of sorrel whiskers hid half his face. The black slouch hat that canted low above one eye threw it into shadow; the other eye gleamed like dirty ice. He wore raggedy linsey clothes and tall moccasins.

"Heerd you all a-singing and whooping it up." His grin showed a mouthful of rotted teeth. "Figured we all would

16

join the stomp.'' Suddenly he raised his voice in a shout. ''Aw right, boys, come on!''

Two riders came through the trees, one leading a riderless mount. They hauled up at clearing's edge. The chunky fellow in the lead said: ''Good going, Perce.'' This one sported a fancy *charro* outfit like a Mexican dandy's, but he was Anglo, yellow-haired and blue-eyed, maybe twenty-seven. His blocky face was bisected by a pair of silky mustaches. A twisted black cheroot dangled from the corner of his lips.

Giving the camp a careful lookover, his glance lingered with mild surprise on Big. He took the cheroot from his mouth and spat sideways. ''What d'you know? Thought I smelled something besides sheep.''

''Yeh, Leon,'' chuckled Perce, ''how 'bout that? Seems we treed us some coon to boot.''

Luis Ayala got slowly to his feet. ''Señor Manigault. You wish for som'thing?''

The chunky man laughed, shaking his head. ''Jesus. Do we wish for something. You ever see the like? All bright-eyed innocence.'' He tipped the cheroot at Luis like a gun muzzle. ''Spick, you got told two weeks back to clear out of this high country. It's all summer range for Lionclaw.''

Luis stood with his feet apart, stubbornly braced. ''No. That is not so. I ask in Morales about this. Is gov'ment land up here. Anyone can use.''

''Not to graze any goddamn woollies they don't. Lionclaw has cattle up here.''

''My sheep don' hurt 'em.''

The third man chirped a sort of weird giggle. ''Hee hee. I wouldn't call the son-of-a-bitch overly friendly, noways.''

Despite a high, nervous voice, this fellow hulked like a silvertip bear. Built broad as a hogshead, he looked bull

17

T. V. OLSEN

strong and hard as nails. His arms and legs swelled like
oak trunks against his filthy linseys. Judging by his matted
sorrel beard and dirty-cold eyes, he was a brother to Perce.
A pair of white peckerwoods if Big had ever seen any.

The dandy-dressing man was a different breed of cat:
younger than either of his companions, softer-looking too,
yet he was the leader here. His fancy clothes and hand-
somely gaited standard-bred horse with its silver-trimmed
rigging were a far cry from them and their ratty-looking
mustangs. He restored the cheroot to his mouth. A thick
and spoiled mouth, touched by a weakness that nicked his
easy arrogance.

"It got said the other time. Sheep and cows don't mix,
boy. Those stinking woollies of yours'll crop this high-
grass range right down to the roots."

"There is plenty grass for all." Luis' eyes were shiny
bright, his voice trembling. But not with fear. "Grass that
sheep eat short will grow all the better in spring."

As if he hadn't heard, Leon Manigault said: "You got
told. What I think, boy, you need a lesson that will stick."
His gaze swiveled to Big. "What's your piece of this, Uncle?"

"Me?" Big spread his hands. "Why, just riding through,
sir. These folks kindly offered me a bite to eat and some
good wine to chase it down."

Perce slouched over by him, holding the rifle loosely
pointed. Bending over, he lifted the wine bag from Big's
hands, heisted it on his forearm and took a swig, then grim-
aced and spat. "Jesus! 'Bout all this swill is fit for, I
reckon. Pigs or niggers."

He threw the bag down on Big's lap. The dog hadn't
ceased his low, throaty growling, and at the sudden movement he edged to his feet, ears laid back.

"Tigre!" Luis said sharply.

Perce laughed. "I'll hesh 'em—" He tilted the rifle up and fired. The dog was blasted over sideways. He lay with legs twitching, his shattered muzzle dyeing the earth.

The savage suddenness of it held them all silent for a moment. Luis' face was dead white under his weathered skin. Big didn't stir a muscle. Didn't even glance down at the wine gurgling wetly out over his knee. His face held bland and unblinking under Leon's stare.

"Well." Leon broke the silence gently. "Just an old-time darkie, eh, Uncle? Know how to mind your place."

Big let the corners of his mouth stretch, framing a grin. "I don't never look for no trouble, sir."

"Why, that's fine, Uncle. Tell you what, now. That your horse over yonder, that big black?"

"Yessir."

"All right now. Right here you're smack on Lionclaw's top range. East, north, south, you will be a long time riding off it. But you go straight west a few miles, you can get off it before dark. That's what you want to do. Keep riding while the light holds. First light tomorrow, you don't wait to enjoy the sunrise, you keep going. Straight west, Uncle. You got that?"

"Yessir. I sure have."

Big rose off his heels and tramped across the clearing to where Tarbaby stood tied to a sapling. A jerk freed the hitch-knotted rein; he toed into stirrup and swung up. A heavy pulse throbbed in his ears; a brassy taste lined his mouth.

Jesus. Luis Ayala was in trouble, deep trouble, it looked like. Couldn't just take a man's hospitality, then ride off and leave him in a jackpot like this one. Yet what the hell else could he do? Against three men with rifles and handguns. And that Perce's rifle steadily following every move he made.

"Goddamn, that's some horse," observed the bear-built peckerwood. "How you reckon this nigger got hold of a horse like that?"

"Never mind, Ira," Leon smiled. "Uncle's got a long ride ahead. Going to need a good horse."

Big reined slowly across the clearing, skirting the watchful men. Luis stood with hands clenched at his sides, his face colorless with a dismayed, silent anger. He wasn't two feet away from his rifle, and now the fact that they hadn't bothered removing it well out of his reach struck Big with an ominous significance.

Sure not. It was a deliberate cat-and-mouse play. They wanted Luis Ayala to go for that rifle. Given the thinnest of excuses, they'd shoot him down as easily as they had his dog. They didn't count a nigger drifter worth sweating over: just wanted him out of the way so they could goad the boy at their leisure. . . .

Jesus, what could he do? Maybe—

"Just hold up a minute, Uncle," Leon rapped out sharply; he pointed at the Winchester booted under Big's knee. "How much you want for that?"

"Uh . . . my horse, sir?"

"Uh-uh, buck. Your rifle." Leon reached in the pocket of his charro jacket; he flipped up a coin and caught it. "It takes my favor, sort of. Give you this nice shiny double eagle for it."

"Well, sir, if it's all the same to you—"

"Let me put it this way." Leon was smiling, but his eyes slitted bright and hard. "Be too bad if you rode out and then circled back here and tried to dust us with that long gun. Then we'd have to kill you. I'd hate like hell for that to happen.''

"Oh no, no, sir. You don't need to worry 'bout that.''

"That's what I think. Perce.''

Leon motioned with his cheroot, and the rangy pecker-wood moved over to Big's stirrup, yanked the Winchester from its boot, and stepped back. "Now,'' Leon said, "come get your money.''

Big had one iron-clad rule of which he'd never yet run afoul: *Keep out of white man business.* Way he figured, you could walk soft around 'em and still follow your own ways. He'd never found it hard, being a keep-to-himself sort anyway. Never pack a handgun, hold a weather eye on the fast-drawn lines of which every black man was aware, and you stayed well out of trouble and still kept enough independence to suit you.

Goddamn. Then why in hell, after years of making the rule work his way, was he set to go fast against it? And why this dead-cold conviction that he hadn't even a jot of choice in the matter?

As he nudged Tarbaby over by Leon's horse, Big glanced at Luis with a grin. "So long, sheep boy. Nice meeting you.'' Snapping a finger against his hatbrim as he spoke, jaunty and unconcerned. Then he was reining up stirrup-to-stirrup with Leon, who tossed him the coin.

Big didn't even attempt to catch it. As the coin spun from Leon's hand, he was crowding Tarbaby hard and side-ways against Leon's mount. Leon gave a choked, startled yell as Big, moving fast, grappled him around the neck. At the same time he grabbed for Leon's pistol, but it was hol-stered on his opposite hip, and Big had to reach around him. Leon was struggling wildly; Big's fingers only brushed the pistol grips.

Just then the horses sidled nervously apart. Both men began to slip from their saddles; Leon clawed at Big's arm. But Big kept his hold; hugged together, they made a single target, and now he heard Perce yell at Ira: "Don't shoot, you damn fool! Watch the spick!"

Big and Leon toppled free of their saddles, falling between the horses. Leon was half-pinned by Big's weight, one foot still hung in his stirrup, and was yelling hoarsely as his body swung to his animal's panicked shuffling. Suddenly Big let go his hold on Leon and scrambled across him to grab at the pistol again. This time he pulled it free of the holster.

In the same instant, Perce loomed above the two, his rifle swinging up. Big scrambled to his hands and knees just as Perce's rifle butt slammed down on his neck. The earth seemed to pinwheel in pain, whirling away from him. Then the rifle butt crashed against his temple. And that was all he knew.

Chapter Two

Lord A'mighty, Buford, what you got yourself into now? The thought caromed wearily across the battering ache of Big's skull as, coming dimly back to his senses, he felt his hands jerked up behind him. Then he came fully, shockingly awake. And was promptly sick, retching thinly against the loam where his face rested. He was sprawled belly down, and now he felt the pressure of thongs biting into his wrists and being yanked tighter.

"All right," he heard Leon say in a savage, shaking voice. "Get him on his feet. Put a noose on his head."

Lord God. They sure-hell weren't losing any time. The two peckerwoods grabbed his arms and dragged him upright. Ira held him that way while Perce fetched a lariat and shook out the coils and dropped the noose end over his neck. Big shook his head to clear it; the scene swam back to focus. Leon was facing him from a couple of yards away, hatless, his fancy charro suit smudged. He was holding a pistol on the Ayalas, but it was Big that he watched. Leon's face was pale with rage, the lips drawn back from his teeth.

"You damn cocky dinge." He wiped a trembling hand over his mouth. "You want my gun so goddamn much— here!"

He took a long step, chopping the pistol up and down. The muzzle raked across Big's forehead; he staggered and would have fallen except for Ira's supporting bulk. Blood showered into one eye; he blinked it slowly away. Hitting him once seemed to clear Leon's temper. A crooked smile fluted his lips.

"Toss that rope over a limb, Ira. Nothing too drastic— yet. Pull him up on his toes for now. High as you can get him. Then tie it down."

Ira gave his loonie giggle as he yanked on the rope and pulled Big stumbling over to a sizable oak. Throwing the rope over a knurly bough, Ira caught it on the drop. Gripping it in both hands now, leaning his weight, he drew the noose choking tight. Big craned his neck back and tightened his throat muscles, but felt himself being pulled slowly up on his boot toes. Giggling, Ira ran the rope twice around the trunk, then made it fast.

Leon's glance moved to Luis Ayala; he pointed at the needle gun. "Go on, boy. Pick it up."

Luis shook his head tightly, keeping his eyes on Perce's ready-held rifle. "That is what you want. No."

"Better go for it," Leon said amusedly. "It'll save that squaw of yours a lot of trouble."

"What you mean?"

"Show him, Perce. Cut a few clothes off her to start with."

Perce nodded and handed his rifle to Ira, who gave him

24

a worried grin. "Hey, Perce. Pappy wouldn't like that no-ways. He will skin us alive, he finds out."

"Thing is, he don't need to. Don't be a goddamn ole woman." Grinning widely, Perce pulled a Bowie knife from his belt and flicked it at his brother's beard, clipping off a strand. "Boy howdy, now there's an edge."

Perce tramped over to Meramee and seized her arm. Twisting it up behind her back, he increased the pressure till her body arched in a bow of pain. Yet she didn't make a sound, not even when he laid the Bowie's razor edge against her throat. Chuckling, Perce reversed the blade edge outward and thrust it inside the neck of her blouse. Pushing downward, the blade cut the fabric at a touch. The parting cloth gaped open, showing the girl's sleek, bronze flesh.

Luis exploded into motion then. But he didn't go after the needle gun. His move caught Leon, ready to cut him down, off guard. Leaping at Perce's back, Luis wrapped an arm around his neck. Ira strode over, grabbed a handful of Luis' hair and pried him away from Perce, then flung him to the ground. Luis rolled over twice before he came to a jolting stop against a wagon wheel. He dragged himself to a sitting position, blood streaming from his nose. A small pack lay by the wheel close to his left hand, and suddenly he seized it and tore at it with both hands.

Leon, just watching, brought his gun slowly level. Big opened his mouth to yell at Luis, but the noose choked his words to a senseless wheeze.

Luis ripped open the pack; his hand dived inside. Blued steel glinted as the hand came out and up. Leon fired. The bullet's impact drove Luis back against the wheel. As he hung there, Leon shot again. Luis' body jerked, then went slack as he pitched forward.

He didn't move again. Powder smoke hung like a golden shroud in the dying light.

"Went for his gun." Leon softly broke the silence. "That's how you saw it."

"Yeh," Perce said. "That's how. No damn reason at all, was there?"

Moaning in her throat, Meramee struggled against Perce's grip on her back-twisted arm. Leon walked over and picked up Luis' pistol, an old percussion Colt. "What do you know," he said. And laughed. "He couldn't of downed a field mouse with this thing. Every chamber's fouled to hell."

"Sure wa'n't no way of telling so," Perce grinned.

He let go of Meramee. She stumbled to Luis' body and fell on her knees, pressing her hands over his bloody shirt. Perce clucked his tongue sadly. "Sure is a hell of a note." Nodding toward Big: "What about him?"

Big's leg muscles hurt with the strain of holding his weight high on his toes; he held his neck tendons tight-ridged against the constricting noose, which was slowly strangling him all the same. He watched Leon turn on his heel and stare at him.

"What do you think? He's a witness now. So's the girl."

"Hell," Ira said nervously. "They's just a nigger and a squaw. Their word ain't gonna tell agin us. Look, Pappy be back from his hunting shortly. We best get back to camp."

Leon's face tightened. "I didn't reckon any Denbow would draw lines. Your pa either."

"You don't know Pappy," said Ira. "That's right, ain't it, brother?"

Perce nodded reluctantly. "Yeh. Ira ain't heavy on brains, Leon, but he is right about Pappy. He—hark."

26

Even Big, his ears popping with the pressure of congested blood, picked up the sound of a horse coming. Moments later a man rode into the glade. He pulled up, his frosty eyes touching quickly over the whole scene, then dropped off his short-coupled billy horse. A towering rawboned man near to sixty, he moved with a mountaineer's light step. His gaunt, leather-colored face was rimmed by a white beard close-cropped to his jaws. He carried an ancient Hall muzzle-loader in the crook of his left arm.

"Come back to camp and you wa'n't there," he said flatly. "Then I heerd a shot up over this way. More shooting jest now. What you boys been up to?"

"Why, nothing much, Mr. Denbow," Leon said easily. "It's that spick we told to clear off a couple weeks back. We ran into him again, as you can see. I'm afraid he wouldn't listen to reason. Went for a gun and I had to shoot."

Denbow's glance swiveled to Big. "Him?"

"He was here when we came in. Just a drifter. Tried to take a hand, so we trussed him up."

"Half hanged him, looks like."

Leon's spoiled mouth smiled. "Not like he was a white man now, is it?"

Denbow gave a dry, cold nod. "Jared Denbow's pulled on a rope or two in his time, Mr. Manigault. Back in Tennessee when I was a younker, we seen nothing amiss in stringing up a darkie now 'n' then, he got too rambunctious."

"I thought you might see it that way."

"Ain't said yet how I see it." Denbow's frost-fire gaze shifted to the girl, crouched by her husband's body and watching them all with stark, wild eyes. "That Injun there

27

with her bosom showing. Who was it bared that squaw's bosom? You, Ira?"

"No, Pappy, no sir."

"Perce—"

A nervous grin jerked at Perce's mouth. "Pappy, now you don't know how it was. You—"

Denbow strode over to him. He cuffed Perce hard with an open hand, staggering him, then hit him again on the backswing and knocked him sprawling. Perce dragged himself up on his elbows, blood gouting from his broken lip. Jared Denbow stood over his son like a gaunt angel of vengeance.

"I warned you times aplenty!" he roared. "The naked flesh of woman is Satan's own lure!"

"Pappy, I swear—!"

"Shut your tongue or I'll kick your teeth out! The sight of woman's flesh is an abomination that leadeth down the road to hell! Particular the flesh of a brown heathen whose tribe liveth as the beast that is cursed in the Lord's eye!"

Lord A'mighty, ran Big's dimming thought, this old peckerwood is loonie as a bedbug. You have bought it for sure, Buford. Couldn't tend your own goddamn business, and now you bought it.... A fierce buzzing filled his blood-swollen head; his quivering legs were on the edge of giving way.

"That's all well and good, Mr. Denbow," Leon said with an uneasy smile. "But right now we have another problem needs tending to. A couple of 'em." He motioned at Big and the girl. "These two have seen what's happened here. They're witnesses."

"So?" Denbow swung him a flat, challenging look. "Heerd you say you defended yourself agin the sheepman."

"Sure I did. But how you think they'll tell it?"

Denbow's snort was softly contemptuous. "You got two white witnesses to the truth. What more you need against the likes of an Injun and this son of Ham?"

"Let's just say I'd like to be sure of 'em."

"Mr. Manigault, you shot this here greaser to defend your life and your land. That ain't killing, that's as should be. But now, sir, I take it you would propose murder."

"How did you call it," Leon said carefully, "when you hung niggers?"

"Them was my green days. The Lord's sent me His call long since. 'Thou shalt not kill.' That there's His commandment, and it don't say no exceptions for them as wear the mark of the beast. Even the nigger and the Injun are shaped in His image."

Jared Denbow pivoted around and walked over to the girl. "Cover yourself, woman," he told her. She stared up at him unblinkingly. Denbow snorted quietly. "Got no English, this squaw. She can't bear no false witness—"

Big's legs sagged; the noose bit savagely. The ragged cut of pain dissolved into a burning that spread from his throat to his chest. Then the scene was funneling away into red darkness; the voices turned to meaningless jumbles of sound that dimmed to nothing. . . .

Next he knew, he was down on the ground on his back. He rolled his eyes to painful focus. The orange leap of the fire washed into his vision first, and then he became aware of the four men standing around him. As their shapes cleared in his sight, he realized the noose was off his neck; Perce was coiling the noose in his hands.

Bending over, Jared Denbow said: "You hear me all right, boy?"

Making an agonized effort, Big raised his head. He

29

forced his lips to shape words. "Mister," he whispered, "I am thirty-five years old. . . ."

Jared's rifle butt slammed into Big's belly. The burning surged back; hot fluid boiled into his throat and he was strangling again.

"You don't sass your betters, boy, not any," he heard Denbow say. "You listen. You mind what's happened here. You mind it so good you don't never show your ugly black face hereabouts again. Set him on his horse, boys."

Ira and Perce dragged Big over to Tarbaby and hoisted him into the saddle, hands still tied at his back. Swaying, Big found the presence of mind to clamp his legs tight to Tarbaby's barrel an instant before Perce lashed his coiled rope across the mare's rump.

Big's head snapped back with her sudden lunge; it nearly unseated him. He held on desperately, hunching his body against her neck, as she tore away through the trees. She cut straight across the meadow beyond, angling into the bunched flock of Ayala's sheep. In the shadow-stretching twilight they resembled great grimy cotton bolls that bounced away right and left, blatting wildly. Tarbaby raced to the meadow's far side and crashed into the flanking timber. Close-packed with brush that lashed viciously at Big's body, it slowed her some. But she could keep running for a long time, he knew, long enough for him to get jolted clean off. He'd always talked to her a lot, as a lonely man did, and he talked now, laying his mouth as close to her ear as he could manage. "Whoooa, Tarbaby, easy . . ." And so on.

Either his words or the dense thickets slowed her to a stop, snorting and stomping. Hadn't been as spooked as she'd made out. "You pick the damnedest times to get playful, baby," Big growled. He sat a moment testing his bonds. *Peales* they were, thin ropes of green rawhide used for tying up cattle you'd worked out of brush. Harder you pulled at 'em, tighter they got.

"She-yit," Big muttered. "You landed yourself in one dandy fix, boy."

He couldn't just sit here in the darkening woods. But he was in no shape to go much farther, and if he left the saddle, he'd never swing his great bulk back on with his hands tied. Nudging Tarbaby gently with his knees, Big worked gradually out of the timber. As it thinned away, he saw a rock-studded downslant of slope ahead. Yet he hesitated before leaving the trees. With the sun gone, he wasn't sure of direction, and he didn't want to blunder back into the arms of those white men. From what they'd said, they had a camp hereabouts. . . .

Sudden bursts of gunfire peppered the silence. Several rifles blasting away at once. Then the piercing blats of the sheep carried to his ears, a conglomeration of dying noises that made his raw gut lurch. The men wouldn't stop, he knew, till the whole flock was dead. That would take a spell, and meantime he could push on.

Carefully Big picked his way down the slope. He was guessing, but he figured if he kept moving this way he ought to hit the creek at a point somewhere below the Ayala camp. He was dizzy and sweating; a savage, battering ache filled his head. His belly was a swelling core of pain, and he could no longer feel his hands. Had best scare up that creek directly, for he couldn't hold the saddle much longer. His vision was spotty; as twilight deepened toward dusk, it was getting harder to make out details of the landscape. But he was pretty sure that by now he'd crossed his earlier trail and wasn't far from the lower creek.

The sounds of dying sheep fell behind him, but the

shooting kept up. Then the shots tapered off, and finally the guns were silent. A kind of hurtful knot in his gut let go. God, what a shameful thing those men had done. The right thing by their lights, that was the worst of it.

Passing over a scantily brushed pasture, he heard a crash of thickets. A handful of cattle spooked away from his path. Then he caught the muffled gurgling of water ahead. Making for it straightaway, he rode Tarbaby out of the brush, down a crumbling shale bank, and into the creek's bright, shallow wash. He was well below Ayala's camp, all right, for the stream, which had gathered deep and slow up above, now plunged down a shale-littered bed, flashing and bouncing in the last daylight.

Wearily Big halted Tarbaby, "Whoa, whoa," and then, slinging his right leg up across the pommel, dropped off on her left side. His legs gave way, and he fell face down in the narrow current. "*Gawd . . . !*" The mountain-fed stream had an icy burn that shocked all his hurts to blazing life. Dragging himself up on his knees, Big dunked his head under once, twice, and again, spluttering. Cleared his brain right off.

Teeth chattering, he sat on the roiling streambed and held his hands under water. Again he fought the ropes, twisting against them with a steady power. Give it long enough, soaked rawhide would stretch. Chin bowed against his chest, he worked his hands with a patient violence. Was likely tearing his wrists all to hell, but he couldn't feel a goddamn thing. All he could find thought for just now was getting free.

Finally a slight give to the rawhide told him it was turning slick and loose. Wrenching hard on the strands, Big felt them slip. He felt a tearing of skin, but only the remotest stab of pain. He wrenched again, his right hand pulling

32

nearly free. A final savage yank and he was loose. He got his legs shakily under him, floundered to the bank, and collapsed there.

Long minutes went by before Big could force himself to move again. Dusk was soaking up the day's heat like a vast gray blotter. As the high country cooled toward night, a rising wind chilled his wet body to the bone. Big rolled to his feet and inspected himself for damage. Jee-zus. He'd caught aplenty. His neck quivered raw to a touch; his throat was so bruised he could hardly swallow. He explored the swollen knots on his skull where Perce had beat him, also the ragged weal that Leon's blow had angled across his face. Pa Denbow's rifle butt had fetched him a belly blow like a mule's kick. His mangled wrists were streaming blood; restored feeling in them brought slicing pain.

Big tramped over to Tarbaby, working his fingers so they wouldn't go stiff. Above all, he needed the use of his hands. Had hurts should be tended. But already his thoughts were boiling beyond the here and now. He had work to do this night. He didn't know or care what precise moment this conviction had come to him, only that it was rooted hot and solid in his guts.

Rest? Hell. He had things to do.

First thing was to tie off his bloody wrists. He managed this with strips of a flannel shirt, which he tore up, using his teeth and half-numb fingers. Wasn't much he could do for the rest of his hurts but wear off their edge with sleep. When he had time for it. The biting chill that knifed through his wet clothes he shrugged away as mere discomfort—the kind he'd survived on many a trail where getting river-dunked and rain-soaked was part of a day's work.

In the saddle again, Big swung Tarbaby back off the willow-choked riverbank and circled up the rocky slope.

He had his bearings now, and a short ride would bring him back to Luis Ayala's camp. A big ripe moon was riding the grape-colored shell of sky; with the light of day gone, it was starting to glow softly across timber and meadow, lighting his way well enough. Big rode slowly, keeping his ears open. He didn't know where the white men had their camp, but it stood to reason they'd bivouac close to water. So he kept wide of the creek, but held along a rough parallel to its winding course.

Hearing men's voices, then a not-close chink of bridle chains, Big pulled into a pooling shadow of pines and stopped. He couldn't make out the riders, but it was easy to follow their progress through the trees off right of him. They were a hundred or so yards away. Coming from Ayala's camp. Then he heard the sounds of halting and dismounting. An orange splash of fire blossomed in the distant timber. Big's lips stretched. Why, that's fine as froghair, white folks. Yessir. Got you pegged just fine now. . . .

He was feeling woozy as hell when the grove where Ayala's camp was located came darkly into sight. The moon swam with a wobbly shudder as if seen through thin-flowing water. Big was shivering uncontrollably; all the mallets of hell were pounding at his skull, and his gut bucked with flashes of pain. Just a little farther, Tarbaby. Jesus. Seemed he hadn't reckoned with how beat up he really was. . . .

Tarbaby began to shy and toss her head, fiddlefooting wildly, as she caught the wet, thick stench of death from the killed sheep. "Whoa, baby! Whoa!" What Big smelled was something else. Woodsmoke. Now he saw it pouring from the grove in a thick pall. Fireshine danced and flickered in the trees. Big heard Meramee's voice rising-falling in a wailing chant, and he almost drew rein. But then, getting Tarbaby in hand, he rode straight in.

They had heaved the wagon over on the fire; by now the whole thing was sheeted in flames. Luis' blanket-covered body was laid out on the ground, Meramee kneeling beside it. Her wild singsonging faded as she watched Big climb down. Dragging one foot after the other, he teetered almost up to the fire and then slacked down on his heels. He was grabbed by a sodden clutch of exhaustion as the beating warmth hit his body. God, that felt good . . . all he could manage for a minute was to close his eyes and soak it up.

Tiredly then, he raised his head and looked at the girl.

Grief? Sure-to-hell grief, about all that a body could stand to feel at one time. Not so much in the silent face of her. Rather in the glossy mass of hair on the ground beside her; she'd hacked it off close to her head in a token as eloquent as any widow's weeds. Beside it, a butcher knife whose blade was varnished with a clotting darkness. Drying oozes of blood patched her sleeves and skirt where she'd inflicted the gashes of sorrow on arms and legs.

For a time there was no sound but the searing rustle of flames and, somewhere out in the darkness, a coyote's feral yelp. Big broke the silence finally, gently. "We all got our ways, little lady. I have buried somebody my own self."

But you couldn't rail against the blind cuts of fate. The kind that had taken Ressie from him so long ago. It was like shouting down the wind. What men did between them was something else. If there was no justice in what life did, there was still justice between men. Should be. But only when a man had the will and the guts to make it so. And if there wasn't a soul but Big Torrey around to stand up for that silent cry, well, by God, that would have to be enough. . . .

Chapter Three

Big was too tuckered to do anything but throw down his soogans near the fire and catch some shuteye. Meramee's chanting started again as he drifted off, but nothing could have prevented him from pitching into a black, dreamless sleep. When he woke, the fire had died to a pile of smoking char. A cold gray light had begun to shred the darkness. He felt stiffed-up and a little groggy, but his head was clear enough. The sledging pain had ebbed to a dull ache, and he guessed his skull wasn't cracked anyway.

Time to get doing what he had to.

Meramee hadn't changed her kneeling position through the night. She was quiet now, but dull-eyed watchful too, following every move he made. Big began talking to her, explaining as well as he could by a mixture of signs and some limping Apache lingo akin to her own tongue that her man would want to be buried in a white man's way. She understood that all right, and he set to digging a grave in the clearing's center, loosening the earth with a stick and scooping it out with his hands, working so fast that he was soon sweating in the shivery predawn. Four feet should be deep enough. When they had wrapped Luis in his blanket and lowered him into the rough trench, Meramee helped fill it and mound the earth over it. Big lashed a couple of sticks crosswise for a marker and stuck it at the head of the grave. Then he bowed his head and tried to think of some words to say.

Hell, he was no padre. Wasn't even a halfway decent Baptist. Had no business making a Papist boy's peace with his God. What he did have was a fair notion of what Luis Ayala had been in life, what life had been to him. Some men you could know for years and never really know 'em; others you could peg dead-center inside a minute of knowing.

Big felt a fresh bite of bitter anger. You didn't ask for very much, sheep boy. Didn't need much. A good woman to side you. A slug of wine. The free wind on your face. Long as you could twang your git box and sweeten the twilight with a song or two and herd them woollies of yourn, you had it all. Never seen nobody so busting with life. Getting so much out of so blamed little. . . .

The gray light had turned to a soft pearling; sunrise wasn't far off. Big prowled grimly around the glade, poking at the smoldering remains of the wagon. He found his old rawhide hat trampled in the ground at the clearing's edge; he shook it out and clamped it on. The men had pitched some of the camp plunder, most of what the Ayalas owned, into the fire and hadn't considered the rest worth bothering with. The peckerwoods must have appropriated the guns, no sign of his rifle or Luis' piece in the ashes, but what about that no-good pistol Luis had gone for when Leon shot him?

Big found the rusty 1860 Army Colt on the scuffed earth where Leon had tossed it. Nearby was the tattered pack that Luis had dug it out of. Rummaging through the pack, Big turned up sacks of shot and caps and paper cartridges. Most of the copper percussion caps were green with corrosion, but he isolated six sound-looking ones. With his teeth he ripped off the ends of paper cartridges till he'd found a half dozen that weren't fouled by dampness. Rolling a hot kettle out of the wagon ashes, he shoved a stick through the bail, carried the kettle to the creek, dunked it, and toted it back to the glade partly filled with water. He stirred up some live coals and got the water boiling, then set to cleaning the fouled chambers of the old pistol.

While he worked, Big wondered what to do about the Navajo girl. Taking her with him was out of the question. What he meant to do next would draw lightning he didn't want striking her.

Mixing more signs with Injun lingo, he got out of her that her father's small band had a village back in the Toscos where they had fled years ago when their brothers had been rounded up at Canyon de Chelly, ending their warlike days. She seemed apathetic, but said yes, she could find them easily enough; the place wasn't over two suns away. The white men had run off or taken the wagon horses, but she could easily walk to where her people were. Big urged her to do exactly that and get away from here promptly, for the white men might come back any time. White man business, he grimly concluded, was nothing for a body with any sense to mess with.

Moving in a kind of obedient apathy, Meramee began gathering up what belongings remained to her, tying them together in a bundle. Her dark glance touched him now and again, expressionless but reflecting her curiosity as to what he had in mind. You have given her a good piece of advice, Buford, he thought wryly, which you ain't got the sense to follow.

He painstakingly loaded the Colt, pouring the black powder from the paper cartridges into each chamber, ramming the .44-caliber balls home with the loading lever and fitting the six percussion caps to the nipples back of the cylinder. He fisted the weapon for heft and feel; it felt all wrong in his hand. Damn, what he wouldn't give to have that good Winchester they'd taken. Few black waddies ever toted pistols; a handgun was a sure invitation to the kind of trouble no black man could afford with his white co-workers. The old cap-and-ball Colt seemed in fair shape for being badly kept, but considering how often these old percussion guns misfired, he'd have given a pretty penny to test it. Only firing it off this near the peckerwoods' camp was out of the question. For the moment . . .

A silver of silvery light was edging the east horizon. He had to get moving.

Climbing into his saddle, Big looked down at the girl. He managed a grin. "Fare you well, little lady. Mind what I said and get walking." He pointed toward the mountains. "That's your way."

She watched him a moment longer and then, without a word, lifted the meager bundle to her shoulders, turned, and headed away through the trees. Big rode out of the grove and swung quickly south along the creek's crooked track.

He'd heard aplenty of the big cattle outfit called Lionclaw. A ruling power in these parts, one that dominated a whole country. A vast and sprawling region whose ill-defined lines straddled mountains and grasslands and desert. Lots of cattle and few people. And the Manigault family, which owned Lionclaw, kept it that way. The Manigaults, it was said, were pretty much a law to themselves, enforcing their claim on rich-grassed federal acres by keeping a tight rein on the business and political doings in Morales, the county seat. And by resorting to gun and rope when necessary.

This Leon, he was a Manigault. The Denbows seemed to be in Lionclaw's employ. Despite their part in what happened last night, Big thought only of the man who had killed Luis Ayala. The Denbows took his orders; would they fight for him too? Catch 'em in their blankets, he would stand a sight better chance of bringing this off. . . .

The faint whicker of a horse reached Big's ears. Pushing in that direction, he soon caught sight of the four horses hobbled out on a belt of meadow beyond the trees. His mouth stretched at the corners. "Well, ain't that fine," he murmured. Stepping to the ground, he tied Tarbaby to a small pine and moved in on foot toward where he had the men's camp placed.

Gliding through the pines, he came to a stop. Voices. Damn, could they be rousting out already? He catfooted through the mouse-gray shadows till a break in the trees showed him the camp. Yeh, they were up and stirring about. Damn. Through the half-screening clumps of pine, he made out a dilapidated tent and somebody sitting on his hunkers laying a breakfast fire. And Leon's voice: wondering in a grouchy, querulous tone if there was a drop of whiskey about.

Old Denbow's reply wore a chilly edge. "We don't keep the abomination of spirits in this camp, Mr. Manigault."

Crouched low, Big edged nearer, holding behind the close-growing scrub till he had a clear sight of the camp.

40

Leon and the old man were standing sideways to him, Jared locking Leon's sullen gaze with a testy one. Ira was just climbing out of his blankets, yawning hugely as he reached for his boots. Perce, squatting by the fire, was whacking bacon into a skillet. Only he and Leon were wearing side-arms. The rifles were well out of hand, leaning against a deadfall at the clearing's far flank.

Giving the situation a quick size-up, Big thought: There'll be no better time. His hand was sweating around the Colt's grips.

"Hell, I'm cold," Leon said surlily. "Just wanted to warm my belly."

"Warm it by the fire. Breakfast will be ready directly."

Big moved sideways and out to the clearing's edge. "Mr. Manigault got no time for breakfast," he said quietly.

Perce wheeled up and around, the skillet falling from his hands. Big promptly tipped the Colt level on him. "I wouldn't move so sudden, mister," he said.

Leon stared at him, then laughed. "Well, well, it's jig time on the mountain. You dumb darkie, that gun is no damn—"

Big tilted the Colt an inch sidelong and fired. The ball whomped into the deadfall. Pale smoke drifted; the shot echoes trailed into a dead stillness. Big eared the hammer back to full cock. "It works for this darkie, white man." He met Jared Denbow's frozen gaze. "Mister, you hear me. I am taking Mr. Manigault with me. I don't want no fight with you or yours."

"Boy," Jared said slowly, "you got plain-out lucky last night. It was my reckoning we had whupped some smarts into you."

"Mr. Denbow, I tell you what. You got such all-fire smarts, you know what an awful mess a bullet makes going

41

through a man. What I think you should do right now is tell your son he ought to shuck that hogleg of his on the ground.''

A pale blaze flickered in Jared's eyes, but it stayed cool and banked. "Do it, Perce," he said in an iron voice.

"Tell you what else," Big said. "You don't touch the gun, Mr. Perce. What you do is uncinch the belt with your right hand and let go.''

Perce was the one who concerned him. Leon's pearl-handled gun was an ornament that shouted authority; it was toted for show alone, barring the chance at an execution like that he'd done on Luis. And Leon's eyes were veiled and cautious now; a tic of fear jerked at his mouth. But Perce's gaze had a high-wild shine. Man who wore a well-kept piece in a stiff holster with a low-slung swagger was a man fancied himself some shucks with it.

Big was halfway sure that Perce would make his try. Yet it came so quick and smooth it nearly caught Big off guard. Perce unbuckled the belt slowly, but even as it fell, his hand streaked back and down, seizing the grips of the still-holstered gun and whipping it up.

Big's cocked pistol was pointed at Perce's right side. He jerked the trigger.

Perce gave a whickering howl, then dropped to his knees. His arm flapped like a scarecrow's; wet darkness sprang across his sleeve.

"*You stay set, old man!*" Big roared the words on the heel of his shot, fast-cocking the Colt again as Jared Denbow took a long step. Jared froze. Big moved in swiftly, scooped up Perce's pistol belt, and stepped back. "Now . . . you can see to him."

Jared pulled his son to his feet. "Lemme see that—" Perce was rolling-eyed with anguish, making little squeaks of pain. "Shut your mouth and lemme see!"

Moving over to Leon now, Big yanked the pistol from his belt. "You." He motioned to Ira. "Get over by your kin."

Ira blinked at him stupidly, balefully. Then burst out: "You goddamn coon! Where you get off shooting up a white man—"

"Mister, *move!*"

Ira lumbered over by Jared. Old Denbow was half supporting Perce and now, yellow-eyed with rage, he looked at Big. "You busted my boy's arm all to hell, nigger. Bone's all busted to hell."

"Well, it's like the old plea goes, Mr. Denbow. What's that favored one you got hereabouts? . . . self-defense. You men stay like you are. Keep your backs to me.

"Go ahead. Just see you don't try nothing else."

Jared dug a dirty bandanna out of his pocket. Skirting around them, Big backed over to the deadfall, picking up one of Ira's blankets on the way. Working fast, he gathered up all their rifles along with Luis' and his own and cinched the blanket tightly around them and all but one sixgun, Perce's. He buckled on Perce's pistol belt, then slung the bundle of guns to his shoulder. Holding Perce's gun loosely trained, he said: "All right now, Mr. Manigault. You pick up your bridle and that fancy hull of yours. We are going for a ride, you and me."

Leon turned his head. His face was white, his mouth twitching. "You're making a pile of trouble for yourself, Uncle, can't you see that? If you're smart, you'll—"

"Why Mr. Manigault, sir, you're talking to a dumb darkie don't know beans when the bag's open. You fetch your saddle, sir. Fetch it!"

As Leon crossed the clearing to where his plunder was

piled, Big said softly, "You hear me, you Denbows. I will be watching behind me. I catch sight of any Denbow face at my back, I will bust it wide open."

Jared Denbow's face was gray with anger; his white-bearded jaw jutted. "You mind what *I* say, boy," he said shakingly. "You have ruint my son's arm for good. You will be seeing this Denbow face afore long. When you do, you are gonna be the sorriest nigger ever trod on a white man's corn—"

Motioning Leon ahead of him, Big circled wide of the Denbows, holding a bead on them till the trees closed them off. Then he urged Leon, stumbling with the weight of his heavy saddle, toward the hobbled horses. "Cinch up, Mr. Manigault. We got some traveling to do."

Leon flung his saddle on his standard-bred. The animal seemed to catch his fear, gyrating away from him, and Leon cursed it. Big threw the hobbles off the three Denbow mounts and fired Perce's gun twice over their heads, hoo-rawing the skittery mustangs into a run. They pounded away toward the north, and Big smiled. That was some half-wild horseflesh for certain; the Denbows would be a spell rounding them up. He freed his own rifle from the bundle of guns and shoved it into his saddle boot, then fastened the bulky bundle to his pommel. Afterward he untied Tarbaby and mounted up.

"Get on your horse, mister. Ride ahead o' me. That way." Big pointed. "Go easy and hang close. This hogleg is gonna be square on your back."

Leon was so shaken that he fumbled the stirrup twice before he toed into it and swung up. "Wh—what are you going to do to me?"

Big waggled his head. "That's a question, ain't it? Let's ride—"

They pushed northwest, Big bearing on a course that would take him deeper into the foothills. Fact was that now he'd taken the first step, he had no clear idea what he'd do next.

There was a sheriff down in Morales, and Big knew where the town was; he'd passed through it early yesterday. When he'd stopped at a saloon for a glass of skullbuster, the barkeep had been so tight-assed snotty about serving him that he'd taken the one drink in a gulp and then cleared out. Most cowtown watering holes had no color bar; man could drink all he wanted in peace long as he didn't belly up next a white drinker. If Morales was such a tight-assed place, he wanted no part of it. But then he'd heard aplenty about Morales before and how the Manigaults owned near everything in sight, including the sheriff and judge.

So you didn't take Leon to Morales. Didn't try explaining to a bought sheriff how a Manigault had murdered a Basque sheepman whose passing wouldn't stir up a ripple in a pond where everyone jumped when a Manigault hollered frog. Most particularly when ole Leon had him two white witnesses.

Sure, justice for Luis Ayala could be gotten with one bullet. He didn't deny that the temptation nested in his guts like a hot, hard kernel. But it softened short of decision. Hell, he was no killer . . . had never even pulled iron on a man in anger. Couldn't straight-out shoot any man. Wouldn't have shot Perce if he hadn't forced it. The thought flickered in his mind that just maybe he could hand Leon his nice shiny pistol and tell him to defend himself. But Big wasn't sure he had stomach for that either.

She-yit, he thought in savage self-disgust. That don't leave a whole hell of a lot you can do, does it, Buford? Except take this Manigault boy up in the wild hills and keep riding. Never give him a hint what you intend for him. Keep him with you long enough to scare ten years off his life, then turn him loose. Maybe you could do worse, considering his state of nerves already. Still, by God, it was puny return for what the bastard had done.

Leon twisted in his saddle, his face shining with sweat. "Be reasonable, will you? Turn me loose now. Ride away, get out of the country. There's nothing more'll come of this, I swear."

Big grinned pleasantly. "Why, boy, we ain't got started yet. You just don't know."

"Listen, Uncle—"

"Which side?"

"What?"

"I say, which side, boy? Your pappy's or your mammy's? Whose brother am I?"

Big kept the grin till Leon turned back front. That's good, boy, get you up a good sweat. You gonna be squoze out like a lemon 'fore you are through. . . .

Dawn blushed up, flooding the land with early golden light and gaunt-flung shadows. The land was climbing steadily, carrying them past rounded ridges almost totally cloaked with taller timber. Big avoided these, threading the swales and passes between them to save time. He had to feel his way into this unknown country, keeping an eye out for stretches where he could start to cover their track. Those Denbows were mountain boys who would hang like leeches even to a cold trail, but they'd be a spell getting onto this one. For the present he could pick his way slow and careful; man could damned easy lose himself in wild back country. But it should be full of likely places to lay up in hiding a spell and live off the land. Big was an old hand at such, and if his captive suffered from the thin pickings, he wouldn't mind a damn bit.

The gentle ridges gave way to rugged hogbacks lifting below the first rise of peaks. Heights that were folded and broken by ancient upheavals, they were barren except for desolate patches of scrub timber. The thin-soiled terrain was littered with broken rock, and now Big began choosing their trail with an eye to hiding it. Pressing Leon relentlessly ahead of him, he looped down a pebbly wash for a couple hundred yards till a steep-flanked ridge loomed to their right. They cut up and onto it at right angles, climbing slowly over treacherous slides of crumbling shale that rattled away from their mounts' driving hoofs. An hour or so of this, Big thought, and their sign would be so confused that the best of trackers wouldn't be able to cut it.

At the summit he halted long enough to slip off his heavy poncho. The high cold was thawing as the sun climbed; Big tipped his hat lower against its slanting rays and secured the poncho to his pommel, keeping a close eye on Leon. Discomfort had sparked up a sullen defiance in Leon; he shivered in his fancy thin-leather outfit and watched Big with a tight, baleful stare. Better get him wore out, Big thought, or directly he'd feel balky enough to kick up a fuss.

Peering down the other side of the long ridge, he saw it was pitched even steeper, fissured with deep frost tracks and studded with rough-angled boulders and loose chips. "All right, boy," he said curtly. "Get you going. Straight on down and go damn easy."

Leon didn't move. Suddenly, hotly, he broke a long silence: "How the hell far you think you can carry this?"

"I'll say when it stops. You do's you're told."

"Sambo, get it through your head you're not hazing just

47

any clabberhead cowhand around! I'm a Manigault. You know what that means?''

"Sure, boy. You're Lionclaw."

"You're goddamn right I'm Lionclaw, and when they get word you taken me, there'll be Lionclaw men swarming back here thicker than flies on a dead mule. They'll find your black ass and they'll hang it higher than your head. No matter what you do to me, they'll get you, by God!''

"I hear you. Get on now."

"Go to hell, Sambo," Leon said in a flat, pinched voice. "You can shoot me now or you can ride me down. But you'll have to catch me first—!''

Whipping his horse's head around on a tight rein, he wheeled the animal hard to his right, roweling him savagely. The standard-bred poured down the ridgeside in a reckless run. The move was totally unexpected, and then Big found his voice.

"Hold up, you damn fool!" he yelled.

But it was too late. Nothing could have halted the panicked standard-bred's straightway plunge as he barreled downward. Leon's frantic yank on the reins only caused the animal's hoofs to skid along the tilting shale. One foreleg hooked in a fissure and then came free as his knees folded; momentum cartwheeled him up and over. Leon's thin scream was choked off as the horse's weight crashed down on him. The standard-bred rolled away and came to his feet, then stumbled the last yards to the bottom and stood there, trembling.

Leon lay twisted and quiet on the sunlit rocks. A stream of rubble rattled down and banked against his body. Silence . . .

"Lord God A'mighty," Big whispered.

Dropping out of his saddle, he clambered down the rug-

ged slant to where Leon was sprawled. Big reached down
to roll him over, then pulled back. No telling without you
touched him what-all had been busted . . . but one thing was
certain. Leon Manigault was stone-dead. The fall itself
might have done the job. Or the horse's crushing descent.
Either way, nobody could have his head wrenched at such
an angle to his body and still be alive.

Big eased down on his haunches and settled his arms on
his knees, hands dangling. A weary-sick wave of revulsion
swept him. Lord A'mighty . . . if he hadn't been wholly
sure before, he sure-hell was now. Nothing short of de-
fending his own hide could have pushed him to take any
man's life, even Leon's. And now it didn't matter. Accident
or no, Leon Manigault was just as dead. And not another
soul had seen how it happened.

Suppose anyone had, what difference? Big knew the
brass-bitter answer to that: It wouldn't count for one sorry
damn. He'd taken Leon away at gunpoint, and the Denbows
would tell it that way.

Accident. Sure it was. Just you give yourself up to their
law, Buford, den you tells all dem white massas as how it
was an accident. Yowsah. You tell 'em and watch 'em
laugh their butts off. Right after they done cutting off your
cojones and stringing you up for buzzard bait. When a
black man can be fetched like that just for being an uppity
goddamn nigger, you figure what chance you got explaining this here away. . . .

What chance he had was the one he made for himself.
Exactly that. One. And that was to get clear the hell away
from here, far and fast as he could.

Chapter Four

Eldon Manigault walked a slow circle of the office, head bent. One hand was shoved in his pants pocket; the other rubbed his forehead in a rotating gesture. He gazed at the adobe walls hung with the trophies of a past in which only the wealthy could afford to indulge a dilettante interest. A shelf of prehistoric pottery unearthed from an ancient Indian camp on Lionclaw range. An Apache saddlebow and a Navajo *bayeta* blanket. A tarnished bronze bit, an iron arquebus, a corrosion-pitted cutlass, all of Spanish origin. Fruits of his interest, of course. His brothers couldn't have cared less. Or their father either . . .

"What's to be done, Mr. Manigault?"

Blassingame's quiet voice jarred him back to the business at hand. As Eldon lowered his hand, he noticed it was trembling, and he shoved it in a pocket. Grief? He wasn't sure just what he felt at the moment. Except numb and uncertain. He swung a reluctant glance to the burly Lion-claw foreman, shaking his head curtly.

"It's not for me to say, Ferd. We'll have to wait on Ruel."

Jared Denbow cleared his throat harshly. The gaunt mountaineer stood in the doorway, his feet braced flat apart. The flat-brimmed hat that Eldon had never seen him remove was clamped low and level, as no-nonsense and uncompromising as the man himself, above his eyes. Eyes that were wintry and impatient and edged with a baffled disdain.

"We don't got a whole passel of time for waiting, sir. You want to ketch the coon killed your brother, you best be hustling on his trail 'thout delay."

Again Eldon shook his head. A young-looking man of thirty, he was tall as his brothers were not. He had his father's height, but not his heft; he was slender rather than wiry. His hair was ash-blond, his eyes a meditative gray; his long-jawed face was clean-shaved and amiable. He was carelessly attired in a wrinkled gray corduroy suit.

"We'll wait," he said. "My brother Ruel gives the orders here."

Denbow gave his head a quarter turn right, never taking his frosty eyes off Eldon; his mouth pursed, his bearded jaw worked as if he were barely damping the impulse to spit. "My boy Perce's arm is busted like a stick. That arm's gonna be stiffed-up for good or I don't know what a ruint limb is. I got a stake in any coon-treeing's to be done."

"I understand how you feel, but—"

"Nigger took our guns. That's all my sons and me need, guns. You give us the wherewithal to fetch him, we'll deliver his scalp stretched on a curing frame. Right here!"

51

Denbow brought his horny palm against the wall with a slap that nearly made Eldon jump. "You can deck this here empty spot with his wool."

Aware of Blassingame's searching glance, Eldon suppressed his disgust. "All very well, but we'll wait. My brother has gone to Silver City on business . . . he's due home early tomorrow. Anyway, it's nearly sunset now— too late in the day to get anything organized and under way. Tomorrow's plenty soon enough."

Denbow's face was flinty and unrelenting. "Till noon tomorrow. We don't wait no longer. You sure he's coming?"

Eldon smiled thinly. "Mr. Denbow. If my brother says he'll be somewhere on a certain day at such and such a time, you can bank on him being there."

"Tell you what you do, Jared," Blassingame said in his deep, quiet voice. "You're plain tuckered from all that riding and trailing. Lay odds you didn't get no sleep last night either. You and your boys catch some shuteye in the bunkhouse. Old Maldenado on our crew, he knows medicine ways. Can set a bone good as any sawbones. You have him look at your boy's arm."

"Ain't no greaser horse-doctor tetching my boy's arm. I have looked to it myself."

Denbow's red-rimmed gaze jarred Eldon with the heel of his contempt. Then he turned on his heel, tramped down the hall to a side door, and went out.

Moving to a window, Eldon glumly watched Denbow join his sons in the yard. Denbow spoke brusquely; they followed his tall, long-striding form toward the corral, the thickset Ira leading their horses. Perce, his face grayish with pain, trailed behind, hugging his arm in its dirty sling. What a prize trio, Eldon thought. Ira, a little better than a witless hulk. Perce, burning with his father's restless energies and kept in leash only by his father's iron hand. Jared himself, directing all of his own brittle fire into an unyielding creed molded by the codes of his forebears.

Scourings of an older frontier, the Denbows had come onto Lionclaw's north range a year ago, driving a jag of miserable cattle. Having decided to sink his stakes on the lush-grassed government acres, Jared Denbow had come directly to Julius Manigault and told him so. "I heerd it said you lay claim to a big passel of land what's public domain," Jared had said. "Heerd you got a way of running off anybody tries to argufy it. I am telling you straight-out I am going to prove up on a piece of it. You want to argufy me, you be set to burn powder on't. I ain't budging for bullets nor barter." At first old Julius had been wordless with amazement at the gall of a ragged mountaineer who'd bearded him in his own den and flung an ultimatum in his teeth. Nobody had talked to him that way in thirty years. And then Julius had given one of his great gusty roars of laughter.

Eldon hadn't been too surprised. His father was given to occasional whims of largess, and he'd always respected raw guts. He'd told Denbow he could build and run his cattle unmolested long as he liked, just so there wasn't any goddamn nonsense about proving up a federal claim. Also, if he weren't too goddamn proud to take wages for honest work, Jared and his kin could go on the Lionclaw payroll as line riders for that north range. Tend his cows with theirs and take care of any trouble that came along, meaning others like the Denbows. Jared didn't give a damn about others, and he had a contempt for legal fooferaw that matched Julius Manigault's; a handshake between men was a binding pact. And the bargain was struck. A shrewd stroke from

Julius' standpoint. His word given, Jared wouldn't expand further, and he would defend that corner of range against all comers. . . .

"Lord," Eldon muttered, "that son of his needs rest and proper looking to. But the old man'll drag him on this chase if it kills him."

"Don't reckon Jared takes his text from the New Gospel," Blassingame said dryly.

"Of course not. An eye for an eye. That'd be the one—" Eldon turned with a tight grin. "Will it be any different with us?"

Ferd Blassingame gave a slight, neutral shrug. His face, craggy and impassive under a shock of pepper-and-salt hair, was etched less by age than by his twenty-five years in Lionclaw's service. He'd state only facts, never his opinions, where the Manigaults were concerned; his loyalty to Lionclaw was absolute and unquestioning.

"I reckon you know the answer," he said matter-of-factly. "Your pa will be hellfire to nail up that darkie's hide. Ruel, he won't have no feeling about it. He'll sniff the idea over from every side and judge what's to be got from it."

"Well, what *I* think is, we're not altogether sure what happened. As Denbow told it, Leon killed that sheepman in self-defense. Then this nigger, apparently a drifter with no legitimate interest in the matter, jumped Leon and got pistol-whipped and dragged off. Leon and the Denbow boys had him hung on his toes when Jared came on the scene. They ran the nigger off. They were half the day rounding 'em up and then they took the trail. It was slow going and they didn't find Leon's body till this morning. His chest was crushed and his neck broken. You saw

Leon's body—no other mark on it. No wound of bullet or knife. What does that sound like to you?''

Blassingame shrugged again. ''Maybe that he took a header off his hoss trying to get away and the hoss fell on him.''

''That's not murder, Ferd. And his body was found laid neatly on a level spot below the ridge, arms folded on his chest, eyes closed. Laid out with *reverence*—by a man who respected the dead. *That's* not a murderer. Whatever that nigger had in mind, it wasn't killing. Hell, he could have done that at the Denbow camp.''

''All right, boy. You tell your pa and Ruel as much. That all?''

''No,'' Eldon said flatly. ''There's the killing of that sheepman. By his own word, Jared Denbow didn't see it. The witnesses were Leon, Perce, Ira, the nigger, and the sheepman's squaw. Ferd, I'd give a pretty penny to know what the latter two saw. What really led up to it? Seems a worthwhile question, knowing my brother and the Denbow boys.''

Blassingame said nothing.

Eldon laughed sharply. ''Leon was a natural-born liar, and you know it. Never told any story straight even when he was a kid. Older he got, the worse he got, wenching, brawling, hell-raising, lying his way out of one scrape after another. He was my brother and he's dead, but there's no sugarcoating the fact. Leon was a master of the facile distortion—and Jared Denbow is a simple man. Julius isn't, yet Leon could take him in sometimes. I'd wager that even those two specimens Jared fathered often pull the wool over Jared's eyes. Yes, Ferd, I'd give a lot to know what that nigger and the Navajo woman saw.''

Blassingame heaved to his feet, hat in hand. ''I reckon

like you said, we wait on Ruel's orders. You going to tell Julius?''

Eldon nodded, a trifle wearily. ''Somebody'll have to. Might as well be me. Christ, Ferd. It's hard to feel anything—yet. Leon and I were never close; we were at odds most of the time. But still—''

''It'll all come out, boy. Give it time. Body can't expect to feel everything at once.''

Blassingame clamped his hat on and went out. Eldon left the office, steeling himself for the ordeal of telling Julius that his youngest son was dead. He went through the hall to the parlor, where Sarita was shuffling about her tasks, sniffling a little. The stout Mexican housekeeper had raised the Manigault boys as she might have brought up sons of her own, after their mother's death. She looked up, wiping her eyes.

''You will tell your pa now?'' Sarita always seemed to read his thought.

''Yes, *Tia*. He must be told.''

''Yes. But you must be very easy about it, Eldon.''

He nodded soberly. Crossing the adobe-walled parlor with its plain, solidly masculine furnishings, he entered the east hall, where the bedrooms branched off. He avoided glancing at the door to Leon's room, where his brother's body lay. Going to his father's door at the hall's end, he hesitated before rapping on it.

''Eldon, Pa.''

''Come in, come in.'' The testy voice had a slurred quaver. Julius Manigault sat in a big leather-upholstered armchair drawn up by the south window gazing across the sprawl of outbuildings and corrals that was Lionclaw headquarters. These days he spent most of his time hobbling around the place grouching about this or that or else merely sitting in his room staring out at the solid symbols of the wealth and power he'd built almost lone-handed. Living bitterly and morosely with the fact that he could no longer handle the reins of his own empire.

"Ruel back yet?"

"No, Pa. He's not due here till tomorrow."

"Ahhh—I forgot." The old man's wasted hands tightened on the chair arms. "Gets harder to . . . come around here, damnit, where I can see you."

Eldon moved over by the window, feeling the sense of painful shock that seeing his father always gave him now, no matter how often he saw him. Just a year ago Julius, at sixty-seven, had still been the big, driving, hearty man that Eldon remembered from his boyhood. Still putting in a full day of hard work, making business trips to faraway cities, wheeling and dealing, enjoying life to the full. Still able to turn the air blue with a roaring of orders, oaths, laughter, and lively stories of how he'd taken this land from Apaches and prairie dogs and tamed hell out of it. Then had come the unexpected stroke that had nearly killed him. A few weeks later, after he'd resumed his old driving pace, a second stroke had left him half-paralyzed and unable to talk.

Slowly, over long months, he had recovered his speech and the use of his legs. But even if he'd been inclined to ignore the warnings of his doctors, Julius Manigault could no longer force his body to a fraction of its former activity. And so, reluctantly, he'd turned over the whole operation of Lionclaw to his oldest son. Ruel's being oldest, he'd made acidly clear to his sons, had damned little to do with it. Ruel was the one who qualified, that was all. Eldon was good for nothing but keeping the ranch books. Leon was good for nothing, period.

"What's ailing you, boy?" Julius demanded.

"Uh . . . nothing."

"Then stand tall and stop shuffling about. Say what you got to."

"It's Leon, Pa. He's—uh—"

"Leon? What's that hellion been up to now?"

"Leon is dead, Pa." The old man was absolutely motionless. Eldon stared at his bright, sunken eyes a moment, then burst out: "He's been killed—"

"I hear you." The withered hands took a clawing grip on the chair arms. "How? What happened?"

Eldon began spilling out fragments of explanation, and then Julius cut him harshly off: "Nigger? A nigger, you say?"

"Yes, but I don't think—"

"A nigger killed my son? You put the crew on that nigger's trail?"

"Pa, no, listen to me now—!"

A wave of blood surged into Julius' face; his trembling arms straightened, pushing his wasted body erect. "You get that nigger fetched!" he roared. "You call in the crew and you tell 'em! I want him *fetched*!"

"Pa, all right, just don't get excited—" Eldon felt a cold alarm at the old man's fury; he tried to press him back in the chair. "I'll give the order, I'll tell 'em, but for God's sake take it easy!"

"*Take it easy hell*!" Julius flung his hands away and heaved to his feet. "Get my gun. Saddle me a horse." He stood swaying like a tall tree; spots of color came and went in his face. He took a step, then another.

"Get my gun," he whispered.

A wrenching spasm contorted his face; his eyes rolled. One hand started up to his head. Then his legs folded. Eldon caught him.

"God—Pa?"

Eldon eased his father's limp weight into the chair. Julius' head lolled; his mouth came open. His eyes were filmed and unseeing.

"Sarita," Eldon called wildly. "*Sarita!*"

Ruel Manigault poured himself a glass of whiskey and walked to the east window of the parlor. For a minute he stood gazing across the sprawling headquarters that had been his father's pride, the glass in his hand forgotten. Seated on the sofa, Eldon and Blassingame exchanged glances but said nothing.

Finally Ruel said without turning his head: "Just what the hell was Leon doing up by the Denbow camp anyhow?"

"Just riding, I guess," Eldon said. "You know how restless he was, being confined to the ranch. He and Perce Denbow were sort of friendly—"

"That's just fine," Ruel said softly. "A pair of itchy punks. Like gravitates to like. I gave Leon strict orders to stay home and out of trouble. Too much to expect, though. Forbid him to go to town and he was bound to stir up mischief close to home. So the sheepherder refused to clear off. We could have still run off one lone sheepman without killing. Now Leon's dead, Pa's dead, and the nigger responsible is on the loose. All because Leon needed a little excitement. Damn!"

He drained his whiskey, swung from the window, and flung the glass at the fieldstone fireplace. The glass shattered to pieces. Eldon jerked upright in his surprise. He couldn't recall seeing Ruel surrender to a violent impulse once in five years.

Sarita came waddling from the kitchen. "Santa Maria, what is that noise? Is something break?"

"Nothing, *Tia*," Ruel said harshly. "Go tend your business."

She looked at him a long moment, turned without a word, and went out.

"Christ, Ruel. You didn't have to—"

"Eldon. Just shut your mouth. I have to think."

Ruel paced slowly around the room, his head down. Black-haired and dark-skinned, he bore practically no resemblance to Eldon. At forty Ruel was stocky and trim, with a hard, square face and bulldog jaws framed by thick side whiskers as neatly trimmed as the wide mustaches that bisected them. He wore a yellow, belted traveling coat, whip-cord breeches, and high-polished boots with a kind of foppish elegance that belied the hard, tensile strength of his body and will. There was no softness or indirection in Ruel: He swept loose ends together with a controlled impatience, plunging straight to the heart of a matter and never swerving from a goal.

He halted and turned, lifting his head. "All right, gentlemen. What we're going to do is get that smoke. Run him to ground however long it takes. However far he runs."

"Ruel, I think that—"

"You've said what you think," Ruel said coldly. "That Leon's death was an accident. And I tell you it doesn't make a goddamn bit of difference. If you'd given the order yesterday, soon as the Denbows brought Leon in, we might have that smoke in hand right now. Jesus, Eldon. Even allowing you're soft in the head, you might have had *that* much sense. You knew I'd give the order myself."

Eldon flushed. "If it was a matter of bringing the fellow in for a fair trial—but that's not what you intend."

Ruel gave a faint, contemptuous nod. "Now, that's astute of you, my boy. That nigger is responsible for the deaths of our father and brother. He's going to pay for them, and I intend to see there's no slipup. Simple as that."

"Bullshit!" Eldon said heatedly. "It's not simple at all! Hell, I'm partly to blame for telling Pa about Leon—bringing on a fatal stroke—"

"Eldon, get it through your head I'm not interested in miring the issue down in a lot of philosophical and circumstantial muck. What the devil would it have mattered who'd told him? Sometimes, I swear to God, it seems you play the conscience of the Manigaults so you can wallow in all our guilts."

Angry and smarting, Eldon sank back against the sofa cushions and gazed sullenly at the floor. You couldn't win an argument with Ruel; he overrode all questions with a ruthless certainty.

"No need to noise this about," Ruel went on matter-of-factly. "We'll do it quietly and without fuss. Get up a party of hand-picked men—not too large a party. Too many would slow the pursuit, get in each other's way, turn surly and unruly if the trail stretches too long. And it could be a long, hard one—"

"Don't see how we can keep word from leaking out," Blassingame said. "The whole crew knows by now."

"Let it leak out," Ruel said gently, "afterward. I want it to. Let the whole country get the story. This fuzzhead killed a Manigault. He didn't get away with it."

Blassingame rubbed his chin. "Might be best to have Sheriff Courtenay head up the party. He can deputize everyone nice 'n' legal. Could raise a fearful stink otherwise."

"Who's going to raise a stink over a dead fuzzhead?"

Ruel said impatiently. "Ferd, you don't get it. This has to be our game start to finish. Lionclaw men. Lionclaw leadership."

"Lionclaw justice," Eldon said bitterly.

A chill smile stirred Ruel's mustache. "That too. Listen to me, both of you. For the past year I've been the Old Man's brain and voice. I've had to handle all the irons he had in the fire. Deal with all the cattle buyers, railroad officials, petty politicos, and whatnot he dealt with to string his little empire together. It didn't matter that the Old Man was crippled and helpless. He was still *alive*. People accepted me as *his* rep. Now he's gone, Lionclaw's like a ship with its rudder cable cut—unless we make it damned clear that nothing's changed. That anybody who tampers with Lionclaw or the Manigaults pays the price."

Ruel strode over to the fireplace and pointed at the big cloth map of Lionclaw's holdings nailed to the wall above it. "There's a half-dozen shoestring outfits back in the Panamint Breaks that are itching to grab our east range. We've kept the fear of God in 'em till now. As many big outfits over west of us would move in just as fast—and any understandings the Old Man had with 'em won't mean a damn." He swung on his heel, hard-eyed. "Let it get out that one nigger spit in our eye and got away with it, we'll have to take on the whole damned country."

Now we're down to it, Eldon thought. There's his reason.

"I reckon," Blassingame said meagerly. "You want the Denbows on this chase? They'll take the trail with or without you."

"All right. And three others. You pick them." Ruel pursed up his lips. "I'll want Vrest Gorman and that Sharps rifle of his. Also a good tracker. Not good—the best."

"That'd be young Lonie Bull. He works ground like an ole coonhound."

Ruel smiled grimly. "Very apt thought. Lonie Bull—I don't know. Isn't he part nigger himself? He looks it."

"Maybe some on his ma's side. But his pappy was old Pinto, a full-blood Cherry-cow war chief. Lonie got raised by the 'Paches; they don't fancy niggers any more'n they do whites. Ain't a man in the territory can shade Lonie Bull on a cold trail."

"We'll need the best," Ruel said curtly. "That nigger has a wide lead already. All right, Ferd, go get the men together. We're losing time."

Eldon said flatly: "Aren't you forgetting something?"

"You mean laying the Old Man and Leon to rest? No, I didn't forget. But someone else'll have to do it; we've no time. You should have had it seen to. You've had time enough since yesterday."

Eldon stared at him. "I'll still see to it," he said angrily. "And damn you, Ruel!"

"You? Oh no, brother. You've no time either."

"Count me out of your damned killing party! I want no part of it!"

"You're coming along," Ruel said in a low, hard voice. "Make no mistake about it, you're coming. Whatever you want to call it, this is Manigault business. Once and for all, you're going to learn what it means to be a Manigault. And if it takes shoving a ramrod up your butt to stiffen your spine, I'll do it, by God."

Chapter Five

Big took a small mouthful of water, swirled it around his mouth, and swallowed. Wetting his bandanna, he carefully swabbed out Tarbaby's nostrils. Then he shook the canteen. A sloshing of liquid pinged lightly against its inside; less'n a pint left.

"Jee-*zus*," he muttered. "This ain't no good, baby. No good atall."

Laying a hand on the mare's flank, caked by a stiffening of dried, dirty lather, he felt a trembling run through her solid frame. He wouldn't have believed it could happen, but Tarbaby was near tuckered out. Those men behind him had just about dogged the two of them into the ground. Sure, they'd started out on fresh horses, and Tarbaby had already been worn by days of steady travel, but Big had gambled that in this hot, rough country the desert-toughened mare could keep ahead of any pursuit that was mounted until the pursuers' horses gave out. Which was

64

why he'd headed into the desert country south of the Pan-amint Breaks . . .

Big had faced a choice back on Lionclaw's high range. He could have pushed deep into the Toscos, gambling that he could lay up in hiding as long as need be. But he'd taken the dead Leon at his word: Lionclaw could put enough men on his trail to infiltrate the whole range. The Manigaults were the power on their home range; all its law, its people, its resources, theirs to command. He'd be hunted by men who knew the country like the seams of their palms. All odds were on their side, and if he got taken, Manigault law would fetch a speedy verdict and a dead-certain one. If they bothered with any law.

First thing, then, was to get clear of Manigault country. And there was only one way to go: south. Try to make Sonora and seek out old friends of his near Hermosillo. Even if the Manigaults' real power was centered in their own county, lawmen throughout the territory would be alerted; Big Torrey's skin wouldn't be worth a plugged cent anywhere north of Mexico. They didn't know his name, that was something, but just the color of his hide would shave his chances lighter than goose down. Any lone nigger showing his face in any town or roadhouse in the territory over the next few months 'ud be asking for an early grave. . . .

So, Big reasoned, he must avoid all contact with people, taking no chances with even the remotest backwoods ranches and hamlets. Make his way undetected to the border across three hundred long, hard, weary miles. A miserable prospect right enough, but it could be done. He hadn't a jot of doubt as to his ability to survive long as need be on the meanest sort of bounty. Man who knew how to find 'em could locate game, greens, and water in the worst country on earth. Might be worn shadow-fine by the time he reached his destination deep in Sonora, but long as he could travel by easy stages, having leisure to forage for grub and water, resting Tarbaby and himself as was needed, he could make it.

Big had counted on that leisurely edge over any pursuit that was organized. He'd have a goodly lead of hours, though he didn't know how many, on Leon's kin. So instead of pushing southward along the easy route that had brought him onto the high range, he'd swung wide to the southeast through the rugged Panamint Breaks, unhurriedly covering his trail by using every dodge that anyone who'd hunted game or wild horses had to learn. You rode hardrock stretches and took to streambeds; you doubled back on your track and zigzagged a broken course. Once he'd left the Breaks, Big was positive that only the shrewdest of trackers could unravel his sign. Take the best of 'em days to accomplish it, and they'd be thrown back largely on guesswork the while.

Well, for guesswork and all, it was goddamn sure those fellows at his back had them one sweet tracking man.

Big had been shocked to awareness of that fact yesterday while he was nooning in a near-dry wash pocketed by a patch of scrawny greenery, which had guided him to the spot. Had seemed a likely place to rest a spell and snare him a few quail. There was some sparse galleta grass for Tarbaby to nibble. After setting up running nooses in the brush runways, he'd dug a small pit in the damp streambottom. Waiting for it to slowly fill, Big had taken the casual precaution of sweeping the horizon with his field glasses. A memento of his horse-hunting days, they were in good shape; he knew how to use them and what to look for. And yet, since he hadn't expected to spot anything, it was blind luck that he'd chosen to halt at the edge of the vast dust-dry *playa* he'd just crossed. He could see his backtrail for miles.

Even then he'd believed that the dusty sign he'd raised almost at once was a sand dervish pulled up by rising currents of heat. Anyway, he'd been in no rush to give it further study. When a quart of water had seeped into the hole he'd dug, he waited for it to settle and partly clear, then hand-cupped it into his canteen a few ounces at a time.

Then he'd again focused the glasses on the alkaline lake at his back, feeling a wintry shock as he picked men and horses out of the funneling dust. *God A'mighty!* How had they done it? Must have 'em some kind of a wizard for sign . . . puzzling out his track this fast.

Throwing his plunder together, Big had mounted up and continued south. But his plan for getting across the territory with a whole hide had been pretty well undone. He couldn't afford the necessary halts to hunt and forage, nor could he take more than snatches of rest. He'd traveled most of yesterday and into the night, finally making a cold brief camp well after dark, rolling in his blankets for a couple of hours' sleep. Before dawn he'd been on his way again, hoping he could get some distance on the posse.

But the first beams of early light had showed the men hanging on his trail. He hadn't widened his lead, and now, by late afternoon, they were starting to close the gap. Big was incredulous. How in hell had they managed *that?* Again he dug out the field glasses and trained them. Blinking his reddened, aching eyes, he could easily pick out the individual riders—they were that close.

So that was how: The bastards had 'em spare horses. They could switch mounts at regular intervals and keep pushing at an undiminished pace—a pace that Tarbaby, saddled with a steady burden of gear and Big's 230 pounds, couldn't maintain much longer.

No way around it, Buford. You gonna have to make a stand. But where? He studied the broken rim of land ahead: a brick-colored desolation of mesas and irregular rocky spires. Plenty of cover of a sort, but where in all of it could a man lay up in such a fashion that he wouldn't be surrounded and cut to pieces in short order?

Stepping into his saddle again, Big gigged Tarbaby into easy motion. A dull burr of exhaustion clung to his brain, and it was no consolation that the men behind him couldn't be in much better shape. In addition to their extra horses, he had noted pack animals laden with provisions and, of course, plenty of water. Just knowing they had their quarry practically in hand gave 'em a pleasant edge.

An hour later they had pulled a good deal nearer, pushing at a fine, brisk pace in hopes they might overtake him before dark. The bastards would make it, too, unless he picked his spot soon. But as long as they weren't in rifle range, Big wanted to avoid running Tarbaby's legs off. He could feel her whole body laboring beneath him; she was holding up valiantly, but her strength was giving out.

Well, Buford, you have wore out your edge, looks like. 'Bout all you can do is make 'em know they have tracked down a coon what's gonna take some killing. . . .

A bullet kicked up a plume of dust off right of him. The booming report of a rifle cracked apart in echoes that clapped across the rocky terrain. Big hauled up in his astonishment, twisting in his saddle. They were still out of good range, yet one man was off his horse and taking shots. Big focused the glasses. Sure enough: The man had set a forked pole in the ground and was bracing his rifle in its crotch.

Another slug whanged off a boulder a couple of yards

away. He was getting the range. Good God A'mighty—
from near a thousand yards away? What kind of sharpshooter did they have, and what kind of gun was he fixed
with?

Big gave a hoarse yell, ramming Tarbaby forward at a
run. Had to find him cover without delay. A big promontory
of exposed rock, sort of a miniature mesa or maybe a
sawed-off butte, loomed about two hundred yards to his
left. If a body could get up on that thing some way, might
be he could keep a party of men at bay for a while.

The prospect had a bleak dead-end feel to it that chilled
his belly, but his last margin of choice had been shaved
suddenly away.

Cutting sideways at right angles, Big pressed as fast as
he dared across the broken ground. The posse would swiftly
close the remaining distance now; already they'd guessed
his intention and were angling toward the promontory at a
headlong gallop. He should get there first easy enough, but
every second was bringing him tighter into that sharpshooter's sights. . . .

Without warning, Tarbaby stumbled and crashed down
on her knees. Big half fell out of the saddle, keeping his
grip on the rein as the mare floundered up. "Whoa, baby!
Steady!" He broke into a trot, tugging her along. She
tossed her head and shuddered, but there was no limp. Big
plunged on at a steady lope. . . .

Another bullet struck somewhere nearby, but he didn't
halt or even glance aside.

Close to the promontory now, Big felt a sinking in his
guts. The flat-crowned height was almost sheer-sided so far
as he could tell. Huge cracks fissured it here and there, but
he saw no indication that a man might be able to ascend it
in a hurry. Then he was in its shadow, the sun's brassy

slant deflected from his eyes. He saw where a whole section of the wall had scaled away, limestone rubble forming a steep ramp to the bottom. The ramp ended maybe halfway up, but above it the wall was split by a great crack that showed clear to its top. Probably it extended to the bottom as well, but slide rubble had filled the lower part.

That was his way up—if there was time.

As he reached the slide, Big scrambled upward without a pause, his legs driving hard at the crumbled rock. It skidded treacherously under his feet, loose chunks cascading downward. Twice he slipped to his hands and knees, feeling the oven-hot flints slash his palms. The second time he fell, he came up limping, but waded onward and up.

Again the sharpshooter fired. This time the bullet sang off stone so near his legs that Big felt the sting of rock chips.

Then the wedge-shaped cleft loomed high and open just above him. An instant later he and Tarbaby were inside it, momentarily cut off from gunfire. In minutes, though, the pursuers would be up close to the slide, and have a clear angle of fire. Big continued up the ramp of fallaway rock, which slanted clear up to the rim. He reached the top and collapsed on his face with a shudder, sweat pouring off him. Dragging himself to his feet then, he pulled Tarbaby back off the rim.

The promontory's crest wasn't as flat as it had seemed from below. Lumpy and eroded, it was laced by jutting pinnacles, many loose and splintered, as if a giant fist had demolished the summit. A sprinkling of bear grass patched the wind-blown soil; here and there a few gnarled, stunted cedars had taken root. Was there another way up here? He couldn't tell right away, but if he could close off pursuit at this point, he might be safe for the moment. . . .

Yanking his Winchester from its scabbard, Big edged back to the rim and sprawled flat on his belly, ignoring the rock's scorching heat as he peered down through the straight alley formed by the fissure. He could see clear to the bottom of the slide; anybody who tried tackling it would bring themselves nicely into range. As he waited, Big studied the rimrock and the sides of the fissure; an idea came to him. But there wasn't time to put it into effect, for the sounds from below indicated that the posse was coming on fast.

The first riders broke into sight.

Just as he'd hoped, several poured recklessly toward the slide, urging their mounts into its brutal ascent. Big almost smiled. Where the slide met the fissure, its passage was so narrow that only one rider at a time could make it through. Four of them were pressing straight up toward the tapered notch; down below, someone was yelling for 'em to be careful. But they kept coming, though slowing down as their horses labored against the steep shattered-rock footing.

Big tilted the Winchester across a slab and drew a careful aim. As his sights crossed the lead rider, he fired. Echoes caromed between the confining walls; the rider pulled up in surprise, unhit. Realizing that he'd failed to allow for the vagaries of downhill shooting, Big coolly levered and fired again, correcting his aim. The rider twisted to the bullet's impact and then spilled out of his saddle, taking a long dive into the rocks.

The other three pulled up.

They opened fire now, but Big was covered as perfectly as they were exposed. His next shot brought a horse down. Its rider stumbled to his feet and started away downslope at a weaving run. Big laid a couple more shots close to the

71

remaining two as they turned their horses in retreat. One horse's footing skidded away and it crashed on its side, the rider flailing wildly away from its fall. The man Big had shot inched to his knees and began crawling sideways to get out of view. His blood trailed a dark ribbon across the dusty rocks.

Big let all of them go, waiting till the slope was cleared off. That would hold 'em a little while, he guessed, and if his idea worked, they might be a sight longer fetching this coon cat's hide than they'd figured. Getting to his feet, he moved forward along the fissure's rim till he came to a barrel-sized boulder about three feet back from it. Some dozen feet down the wall of the notch, a rugged spur projected; it looked rotted as hell. He hoped it was.

Laying down his Winchester, Big put his shoulder to the rock and heaved tentatively, testing its weight and looseness. It teetered gently forward and settled back. Digging in his toes, Big threw his full strength into the effort, feeling the heavy stone sway back again; rock rasped on rock. The boulder had shifted maybe an inch.

Big straightened up, flexing his fingers open and shut. He set his bloody palms flat on the stone's sun-blistered side and called on his reserves of failing strength. His muscles bunched into solid ridges; he felt them swell and crack. A burst of throbbing blood filled his head; a blinding wash of sweat stung his eyes. The rock stirred and grated, budging in tiny jerks.

Then it tipped suddenly outward. As it did, Big dropped swiftly on his side; otherwise he'd have gone over with it, for the rim sloped dangerously at its brink.

The rimrock trembled to a stunning crash as the boulder shattered the projecting spur below it. Big scrambled blindly away from the rim, for the whole wall had appeared faulted, as if one solid tremor might bring it down. Sprawled flat, he listened to massive chunks of limestone thunder into the notch. The din of falling rock kept up for a half minute. Then there was a trailing silence. . . .

Big got shakily to his feet, sleeving his eyes clear.

The rimrock was still intact, but a godawful lot of rock had smashed down into the narrow gulf. Skirting quickly back to the end of the fissure, he took a full sight of the results. His cracked lips winced into a grin. A good piece of the ramped notch was crammed with six and more feet of sizable rubble. Where the crack tapered to that narrow wedge that only one rider at a time might have negotiated, it was now blocked to the height of two men.

A man afoot might climb up and over it, but it would take him a little while. And directly his head topped the mass of rubble, he'd be an easy target for a rifle up here.

Big catfooted over to the main rim of the promontory and peered down. He counted ten men, off their horses now and gathered around the one who'd been shot. He swept the group with his glasses. Old Jared Denbow and his sons were among them, as expected. A dark, stocky man seemed to be giving orders, and now he and a couple others climbed aboard their horses and began to ride a wide circle around the promontory. They'd be looking for any other possible ways of ascent, and Big knew he'd better do the same.

Fading back off the rim, he made a slow circuit of the stumped-off rise. The rimrock was furrowed by erosion on all sides, and he didn't want to risk the weight of his body on it; he was also wary about exposing himself to the guns below. Here and there, however, he inched onto solid-looking ledges where he could command a wide view of the drop. So far as he could tell, it was practically sheer all

73

around. Deep fissures like the one he'd ascended were frequent and so were fans of slide rock that had sloughed from the promontory and heaped up around its base. But he saw no other lucky conjunctions of fissures and slides such as the one that had enabled him to get up here. . . .

Once he heard a shout from below as the circling riders spotted him. Big put a thumb to his nose and waggled his fingers, though he knew they probably couldn't make out the gesture, and then dropped back from the rim before anyone could bring a gun to bear.

But his thoughts were tight and heavy as he tramped back to where he'd left Tarbaby. Sure, he was safe long as he could hold out. All he had to do was camp at the head of the slide fissure and pick off anyone who tried climbing over the pocket of debris. Even darkness wouldn't cover anyone who made the attempt, for they couldn't manage it without rattling all that loose stuff, and he was a light sleeper.

Other than that, he hadn't one damn thing to crow about. Those fellows had plenty of food and water. He was down to his last scraps of jerky and his last pint of water. Most he might hope to scratch up on this barren eminence in the way of grub were a few edible roots and a lizard or two. And of water, the real need, not a drop. When it came to a question of who could outlast who, there was no question at all.

Maybe just one. Whether he stayed bottled up like any cornered coon till he was too weak even to lift a rifle. Or whether he forced the final issue and went out like a man.

Big dropped a hand on Tarbaby's drooping, dust-caked neck. "We're in a hell of a pickle, baby," he murmured. "But I tell you one thing: When they get this coon cat fetched, there's gonna be a few of them massas in the cold, cold ground."

Chapter Six

Sunset bled onto the rim of the desert like a flat stain, sheeting the redrock terrain with pink flame. Eldon Manigault sat on his heels by a fire, swigging strong coffee that puddled like molten lead around the unsettled supper in his belly. He gritted his teeth and stubbornly drank some more, remembering how his father would jeer his squeamish times. "Just like your ma," old Julius would roar. "Get up a mess o' fluttering fantods over nothing atall."

Nothing at all, Eldon thought bitterly. Just a little business of tracking down and killing a man who may be innocent of any wrongdoing. My God, we don't even know his name. He's merely "that nigger." As if taken by itself, that makes everything all right.

He and Ruel sat at one of a cluster of fires that faced the clogged fissure, a couple of men tending each one. Couldn't know but what the nigger might try sneaking down after dark. If he did, the far-reaching glow would catch him sure.

But Ruel's square face barely masked an abstracted irritation.

It's getting to him too, Eldon thought with an obscure satisfaction. Ruel hadn't figured that hanging up one black man's scalp would prove such a nuisance. Weren't all the odds they could muster weighed against him? In spite of it he'd kept ahead of them through three tough days of tracking him, and a fourth grueling day of staying at his heels. Only Lonie Bull's uncanny ability to hold a trail had brought them this far.

"Don't see what you're so damned edgy about," Eldon said innocently. He knew that every hour they just sat and waited was a drop of acid eating at Ruel's driving, impatient nature. "We have that ole black boy sewed up, haven't we?"

Breaking a stick of greasewood between his strong hands, Ruel flung the pieces in the fire. "And are stuck fast waiting him out," he said in a low, savage tone. "Goddamnit, we can't afford the time it'll take to starve out that damn smoke."

" 'As long as it takes,' I thought you said."

"Hell, getting him shouldn't have taken us this long! We've other business to attend to."

"Why don't you relax? You left Ferd holding down the ranch—"

"You know why," Ruel snapped. "Now the Old Man's dead, there are a hundred loose ends that have to be tied up, matters that require my attention. Ferd's a top ramrod—that's his limit."

"All right," Eldon said reasonably. "The nigger's trapped, isn't he? *That* doesn't require our attention any longer. Suppose we get back to Lionclaw and leave some men here—"

A wicked glint touched Ruel's glance. "Oh, no," he said softly. "You're not getting out of it that easily."

Eldon smiled thinly. "I know, I know. It's Manigault business—we're going to see it through to the bitter end, both of us. Well, you can't have it both ways."

"We'll see about that," Ruel said doggedly, flatly. "See what Lonie Bull says. Maybe we won't have to wait—"

Eldon rubbed a palm over his tawny scrub of whiskers. He winced. Four days of naked sun had boiled his fair skin to a lobster hue. The sweat-fouled grit of his clothing chafed his hide with every move he made. His soft muscles twitched with raw aches; his saddle had massaged his thighs and buttocks to a mass of fiery sores. He was so badly out of condition that it would take days more for him to harden out.

He felt a wave of unreasoning hatred for Ruel.

A twist of wry honesty, though, made him admit that it wasn't really Ruel. Or a compounding of physical miseries. Or even the angry humiliation of letting his brother drag him along on a mission for which he had no stomach. It wasn't, in fact, anything except a scalding contempt for his own lack of backbone.

But then he never had stood up to Ruel, not since they'd been kids. Then, being the oldest and biggest, Ruel had always forced a fierce physical domination on his brothers. With Julius' full approval: "Might make men out o' you two," the Old Man would say. Leon had fought back at least, getting bruised and bloodied, but never ceasing to rebel in his wild, sullen way. While you, Eldon thought bitterly, never found the courage even for that. . . .

Jared Denbow came tramping up, his face bleak and forbidding. "I want to ask you one thing. How long are we gonna sit about like lumps on a log?"

77

Ruel eyed him coolly. "What do you suggest? We all charge up into that nigger's gun one at a time and get picked off like jackrabbits?"

"Be dark soon. That ought to cover a man."

"Actually," Eldon put in idly, "he drove back four of our men without picking 'em off. And he had every chance."

Ruel's jaw knotted, but he didn't look at his brother. "You're not thinking, Mr. Denbow. He can still hear you. And you'll have to go to him, he won't come to you."

"He's got to sleep sometime."

"Perhaps," Ruel said sardonically, "you'd like to stake your life on when that'll be. Whether he's asleep or awake, my friend, you'll make too damned much noise. But if you want to take the risk—"

Frosty-eyed, Denbow shook his head. "I reckon I can wait. That black rooster's head is square on the block now. Just a matter of lopping it off."

"Exactly. It may come sooner than you think. . . . How is your boy's arm?"

"Throwing bits o' bone. I don't like the look of it."

The mountaineer turned abruptly on his heel and strode away. Ruel tossed more wood on the fire. "The old fool shouldn't have insisted on bringing Perce along."

"I can tell it really gets to you."

"Eldon," Ruel said gently, wickedly, "I've swallowed about all of your smart-ass needlings I care to. Now keep your goddamn mouth shut, will you?"

The last glow of sun was fading to a plum-colored dusk. Eldon listened absently to the murmur of men's voices around the fires. They were all tired and mildly griping, but there was no mutinous note to it. Not with a bonus amounting to two months' wages being given every man who accompanied the hunt. Besides, tracking coon was sort of a holiday, by God. And you got paid, too.

In the slow-seeping dark, the fires made spreading splashes of orange glare. It glistened on Vrest Gorman's egg-bald head as he walked slowly back and forth, always watching the skyline of the promontory. Vrest was tall, gangling, loose-jointed; his eyebrows and whiskers were so pale that he looked altogether hairless. His bleached eyes were sharp as a hawk's and just as dispassionate. If he had any passion other than the Sharps Big Fifty he carried like an extra appendage, Eldon didn't know what it might be.

Vrest Gorman was a man of mystery. He never talked about himself. In fact, had no interest in talk; he merely took orders. Ruel had told him to keep a watch on the rimrock for as long as the light held. If the nigger showed his head, to blast it off. Vrest could easily do it, with his telescope sight and unerring eye—a fact of which, after today, their quarry had to be well aware. . . .

Emerging noiselessly from the dusk, Lonie Bull came up to the fire and squatted down by it.

"Well, how's it look?" Ruel asked.

"I look the wall over every side. She run mostly straight up-down."

"I know that," Ruel said impatiently. "Is there any other place but here that a man might get up it?"

" 'Pache or white?"

"What?"

Lonie Bull shrugged. A small copper-skinned man, he was spare-built and wiry, agile as a cougar. His drab clothes had the hues of desert dust; a faded red headband, memento of a year spent as an Army scout, confined his straight black hair. Lonie's broad, primitive face was battered and scarred, making him look older than his twenty-five years.

He could remain motionless for hours, but the black obsidian chips of his eyes never rested. His regular job was both rough-breaking and gentling all of Lionclaw's horses. About the only thing he couldn't track was a bird in flight.

" 'Pache climbs anything if there is holds enough,'' he said. "Prove manhood that way. You ask me can a white-eyes climb it, I tell you no.''

"All right. Can you climb it?''

"I bust horses for you. I track for you. That's what I get pay for, eh?''

"Money—'' A corner of Ruel's mouth lifted. "If that's all it's a question of—''

Lonie shook his head very slightly. "You want me climb up there to fetch the black man. I don't never hunt for bounty on man.''

"Well now,'' Ruel said easily, "nobody's asking you to kill anyone. Thing is, he won't expect any visitors from behind—now will he? Don't tell me you couldn't take the fellow alive.''

"I tell you something, Mr. Manigault. One way I don't take the black man; I don't take him light. I never track nothing so trailwise like him. He think out his moves like fox with man brain.''

"He's not the fox you are. Hell, you've proved it. He can only watch one side at a time. And this is the side he'll watch. You can do it.'' Ruel paused. "For five hundred dollars you can do it.''

"Maybe,'' Lonie Bull said. "Maybe I can.''

A wind stroked the height of land like a cool blade. Big hunkered in the lee of a rock, hugging his soogans around his body. It was too exposed a place to spend a night in comfort, but that was the least of his worries. Now that full darkness had obscured the skyline, he'd moved up by the rim to where he could see over it. The island of fires below threw a wide wash of light across the scene, picking everything out pretty well. Men sat around the fires; some had rolled into their blankets. Should be catching a few winks of shuteye himself, but tired as he was, Big felt too tight-wound.

Lord God A'mighty. He'd always been an easygoing cuss, a man to walk wide of trouble. What had brought him to this? Sitting up on a lonely hunk of rock waiting to die?

Couldn't wholly spell it out, even to himself. Justice, sure, but when had justice been such a crying concern to him?

Hell, he'd never been a thing but footloose and no-'count till he'd met Ressie. Tall and toast-colored, lovely and lithe, with a throaty voice that sort of hummed and whose memory could still barb him unbearably. A free-raised quadroon from New Orleans, Ressie had come West to escape a past he'd never asked her about, setting up a little dressmaker's shop in Gilman, Big's favorite stamping ground. There'd been fire struck between them on first meeting, for which he could see his side right enough. What Ressie had seen in a big ugly busted-faced galoot like him he'd never known, but hadn't questioned his good fortune.

Big had been a mustanger in those days. At twenty-four he was still limber-boned enough to rough-bust the wild ones he caught, selling them to local stockmen. It had been a well-paying operation and soon, putting their savings together, he and Ressie had been able to marry, buy a small cow outfit, and hire a few half-breed waddies who didn't mind taking orders from a black boss. Three good years there'd been. And two babies. Roots that were solid-sunk, a mortgage paid off, a touch of prosperity, and hopes for still better years. Then the siege of typhus, which had swept away Big's little family overnight. The year that had followed he didn't like even to think about. After selling the outfit, he'd drifted for a long time, living his days and nights in a haze of whiskey, often falling-down drunk, never quite sober. When his money was gone, he'd quit drinking. Simple as that. And slowly time had scarred and deadened the hurt.

For the past eight years Big hadn't cared for much of anything. But he hadn't reckoned that was so bad. Free-wheeling ways never hurt a man. It was caring that cut to the bone. As he'd figured it, Ressie had raised him above himself and filled him with a determination to do for her, then for the kids. Wouldn't have been all that caring if not for Ressie. Not that he had any regrets; those three good years had been worth a man's lifetime. Just that he'd figured those same years had used up a good piece of his manhood.

Seemed he'd been wrong. Buford Torrey still had more grit in his craw than was good for a man. So here he was with his black tail plunked on a cold rock waiting to die. Maybe, he thought, a man could pick a sight worse way to go. But that ain't much comfort, Buford, is it? . . .

A moon that was thinning toward last quarter faintly silvered the rugged top of the promontory. Wasn't much to be made out except the stirrings of scrub cedars where the wind combed them. All the same, an instant of old habit kept his senses honed sharp to the night. Not that he was looking for anything to happen. Damned little was going on in the camp down there. Once in a while a man might get up and walk out of the firelight, to fetch wood, relieve himself, or whatever. But Big didn't bother to keep close track of their comings and goings. All he had to keep an eye peeled on was that bottled-up slide; where else could they get up?

As he'd easily turned back those four who'd made the try, it would be only good sense on their part to wait him out. Wait for him to attempt the break which, sooner or later, simple desperation would prod him into. Likely sooner. Tomorrow's sun would turn this tall rock into a scorching lid of hell. The couple good swallows in his canteen might carry him through a single day. And then . . .

Tarbaby snorted quietly and swung her head. Her pricked-up ears twitched. The moonlight showed her clear enough from where Big sat. The mare was hobbled in a little hollow a ways back from the rim; a few hours' rest had restored some of her mettle.

It was a little thing, that signal of Tarbaby's. But enough to wipe everything else from Big's thoughts. He'd learned to read her signs so well that they were clear as speech. Right now she was saying that something lay amiss in the night. Maybe in the wind that feathered in a silent west-to-east current across this stony stillness.

Big's spine tingled. Wasn't a damn thing up here but Tarbaby and him, rocks, and a few scrub trees. Nothing to trouble in all that. Yet Tarbaby had picked up something. He knew it with a certainty that ranged beyond his own straining eyes and ears, which told him nothing.

As quietly as he could, Big eased the soogans off his shoulders and reached down to pick up the rifle at his feet. He made no other move. Just listened. Wasn't no way a man could get up here—or was there? Not all the men in that posse were as dumb as the quartet who'd tried to charge up earlier. At least one man had been smart enough to follow a cold trail that Big had believed he'd laid so well nobody could unravel it.

Well, all right. Might be he could do that party, or whoever, one better.

Laying down his rifle now, Big tugged off his boots. Then he gathered up his soogans and, noiseless in his sock feet, moved over to the moonlit hollow where the mare stood. Again she lightly snorted. He clamped a hand gently over her muzzle, whispering, "Quiet down, baby. Quiet. . . ."

A tremor ran through the mare; her head tipped west again.

Taking care not to rattle so much as a loose chip, Big prowled softly around the hollow, hunting for sizable rocks. These he gathered up one at a time and deposited each in the center of the open hollow. When they formed the rough shape of a man's outstretched body, he loosely arranged his blankets over them. Afterward he glided back to his former position and picked up his rifle, then snugged himself on his hip and shoulder against a pair of rocks. He took off his hat and sighted down a niche between them.

The minutes seemed to stretch out endlessly.

Tarbaby, never one to hold still long, grew restless again. The stalker would pick up her small noises. And he would be the soul of patience, moving in by degrees and listening as intently as Big himself. Only you got to come to me, man, Big thought with a cold satisfaction. Don't matter how long it takes, it's you got to make all the moves. . . .

Big had no way of tracking time except by the shift of moon shadow and the growing cramp along his side where the cold rock braced it. But he never stirred a muscle. Man who could stalk like this one, directly he was close enough, might pick up even a whisper of cloth. And Big, straining his ears, heard nothing at all. But the bastard wasn't invisible. He'd have to show himself.

And finally he came, a flicker of shadow among the shadows, moving in utter silence through the boulders. Big made out his silhouette: a slight and squatly built man, hatless. As Big dropped silently into the hollow, he saw a glint of moon on a drawn gun. The man bent by the soogan-covered mound—and seemed, in almost the same instant, to realize the ruse.

He sprang upright again, his eyes wheeling against the shadows.

"Right here, brother," Big murmured. "Case you can't make it out, there's a rifle looking dead at your head. You just leave that iron fall."

The man froze still. Then he dropped the gun. Big edged out from the rocks and tramped over to him. He jammed the rifle under the man's chin, then lifted a knife from the man's belt sheath. "Turn your face to the moon a mite—that's it. Well, I be damned. A honest-to-God ol' broncho 'Pache. Leastways you got the look. How many more they got like you?"

"Just me."

"Yeh, bet that's so. They don't grow 'em like you just for the picking. What's your name?"

"Lonie Bull."

"Well, Lonie, mine's Buford Torrey. Big, they call me. Least you can do if you're gonna make game of a man is know his name. How much they paying you to fetch me?"

Lonie Bull didn't answer. Big jammed the rifle muzzle harder against his throat. "Boy, this here is ready to go off. Just a move by you or a touch by me 'ud do it. Now you talk up."

"I work for Lionclaw. They give two months' pay every man who come on hunt."

"Well, well. And I didn't reckon my hide was worth two

cents. Climbing up here to put a bullet in me, how much they pay you for that?''

Lonie hesitated. ''Five hundred dollar. But I don't come shoot you, black man. I tell Manigault I only take you alive.''

''Do tell. Then hand me over to 'em, eh? What you think happens then; I get spanked and sent home?''

Lonie Bull shrugged.

''Well now, you are prime stock for sure. If that face o' yourn ain't got a touch o' the tarbrush in it, I don't know shucks. Who was the nigger in your woodpile, Lonie?''

''Ain't no goddamn business of yours.''

''Yep, I make you a bird o' many colors, Lonie Bull. Where you get a nice white name like that? Mission school?''

''Maybe you get yours on the old plantation.''

Big chuckled. ''Boy howdy, they learned you a few things at that school. But you don't get salty with me, boy. Not while I hold the gun. Tell you what now. You show me the place you got up that cliff. Then we'll see what's to be done.''

''It don't do you no good.''

''You show me anyway.''

Big prodded Lonie ahead of him. They clambered across rocks lit by a soft moon shimmer, and finally they stood on the promontory's far side. Lonie pointed. Big motioned him to stand off a ways, then peered down the long drop.

Jee-zus! It was almost sheer to the bottom, though the moon picked out knobs of projecting rock and shadow-seamed fissures. Briefly he wondered if Lonie had steered him wrong, but scanning the cliff carefully right and left, he decided that yes, this was likely the best spot. Big knew of the Apache rite where, to prove manhood, a youth must scale a dizzy height, cast *hoddentin* to the winds, and pray to the spirits to bless his *tzi-daltai*, his personal amulet, while he fasted for two days—after which, weakened by hunger, he was expected to manage a descent. But Jee-*zus!*

"You think you get down that, black man?"

"Just you hush a minute, boy. I'm studying on it."

Pretty bleak studying, anyhow you sized it. At least crawling up, Lonie Bull had had faint moonlight to guide his holds. Climbing down 'ud be something else. Man'd have to feel his way with his feet, no matter how well he studied the descent beforehand. Also, he was a hundred pounds heftier than Lonie. Also he was no Apache.

Still, there might be a way. . . .

"Well, Lonie, I'd say you had a sight more learning in your time than just mission school. Now let's hunker down and palaver some. You make tall medicine for black brother, eh? You tell me about them gents down there. All you know about 'em."

Lonie didn't move. "What you do with me?"

Big grinned mirthlessly. "She-yit, boy, what you think I ought to? You're their tracker—ain't you? You're the one got 'em salting my tail."

"I do my job."

"She-yit, your job! Blackbirding for white men's your job. Well, you don't need to worry none, Lonie. I'm like you one way; I ain't no killer. You got my sign straight back there; you know that's so."

"You go down there by and by?" Lonie nodded at the cliff.

"If I can."

"You don't make it. Break goddamn neck."

"Say I do make it, Lonie. What then?"

"You let me live and you get away, then I track you

some more. I lead 'em right to you by and by.''

"Yeh, that's so, ain't it? You just got to take your chances, man. Take my word I don't kill you. But I tell you this. You don't talk up like I want, it ain't gonna help your chances none.''

Lonie dropped to his haunches, and Big squatted down about ten feet away. He listened carefully, sorting out the sense of Lonie Bull's broken-English speech, sometimes inserting a question. He learned about the two Manigault brothers and the kinds of men they were. About old Julius Manigault's fatal stroke. About Vrest Gorman, the man whose deadly eye and gun had come near doing for him. And other things, too, that might prove useful.

"All right, Lonie. That'll do." Big rose to his feet, motioning with the Winchester. "Let's get back to my horse."

"You take horse down with you?" It was a stony-faced gibe.

"Nope. Need my rope."

"Rope no good here. Way short."

"Well, I tell you, Lonie. You made it up with no rope at all at this place you kindly showed me. Seeing's I got nothing to lose, I'd as lief fall down a cliff as get shot or die o' thirst.''

"You get down, black man, you don't get far with no horse.''

"You leave me worry 'bout that." Big paused. "I'm gonna leave you tied up with a gag stuffed in your mouth, Lonie. Can't have you raising no ruckus. But that's a favor, I figure. Better'n a bullet.''

"*Enju*," grunted Lonie Bull. The terse Apache response usually meant almost anything.

"Favor oughta be worth a favor. That Tarbaby horse

means a heap to me. Be obliged you take her for your own and look after her.''

"I think mebbeso you are *loco*, black man.''

Big laughed, deep and easy. "I'm a man, Lonie. That's all. But I know who I am. Hope you find out the same one day. Now you get along—''

Chapter Seven

Tearing up an old shirt of his, he used twisted strips of it to tie Lonie Bull hand and foot. Stuffed more strips in Lonie's mouth, jammed a stick crosswise between his jaws, and then tied it in place with a strip circling the back of his neck. It was a brutal gag, but he couldn't take a chance on the Apache making the least sort of outcry; sound would carry like hell from up here. Then he said a quiet good-by to Tarbaby, sliding his hand over her muzzle. Jesus. Hard a thing as he'd ever done, abandoning the mare. Man oughtn't to get caring too much for anything, Buford, ain't that what you always said? Like a whole heap of other grand thoughts that never jelled in living. You'd owned horses before and you might, given the devil's own luck, live to own others. But there was only one Tarbaby. . . .

Carrying his rifle, boots, saddlebags, and his coiled rope, Big tramped back to the flat shelf overlooking the place he meant to descend. Peering down, he tried to pick out likely holds for his hands and feet, but the misty moon didn't show much that was helpful. He'd have to tackle the descent blind, trusting to Providence, his muscles, and his good rope. And that without delay. More time that went by without some sign from Lonie Bull, the more suspicious the men down in that camp would get.

Big chose an abutment back off the rim, a rounded knob that wouldn't saw the rope, and fixed his noose to it. Then he dropped the coils of his rope over the rim. Its end dangled less than a third of the way down the cliff. Sweat broke on his palms as he inspected the rest of the drop. It sloped off somewhat toward the bottom, but passing the middle part, depending wholly on his hands and feet to support him, would be the ticklish part. Every ounce of weight he could slough would be a help.

He slung his rifle to his neck by a strip of twisted cloth he'd fastened to the barrel, letting it hang down his back. Afterward he dropped his boots and saddlebags over the rim, took a solid grip on the rope, and tested his noosehold by leaning his weight. Then he slipped backward over the rim, descending swiftly hand over hand. In no time, it seemed, his feet dangled free at rope's end. From here on it was hug the cliffside and dig in with fingers and toes.

Carefully Big sought out holds for his feet and hands before letting go of the rope entirely. Then he squirreled downward by painstaking inches, feeling out every crevice and knob before trusting it to his weight. His muscles ached with strain and tension; he wouldn't dare look down even if his eyes hadn't been stung half blind by a salty wash of sweat. His chest rasped painfully against sharp projections; his calloused hands grew slick with sweat and then with blood as they were lacerated by his tight holds on saw-edged stone.

91

He had a bad moment when his groping feet couldn't locate anything but a bulge of smooth rock. Taloned over a couple of precarious holds, his raw fingers grew quickly numb. In seconds, unless he could ease the pull of his weight on them, they would tear loose. Moving himself sideways offered his only chance. Slowly and blindly, he edged to his right, luckily finding fresh grips for his weakening hands. Then his right foot hooked in a shallow fissure and he could pause, letting his arched toes take most of his weight while he worked feeling back to his fingers. . . .

Big inched gradually around and past the smooth bulge. Once he was below it, he found the going a lot easier. Having achieved a definite outslant of the cliff then, he dared look down. He wasn't over five yards from the bottom. Yet it still seemed like a young eternity before he stood once more on solid ground, his legs rubbery and trembling.

He'd have liked to drop flat and just press himself to the blessed earth a spell, but it'd be a luxury time wouldn't permit. He was still in a pretty fix. Directly those fellows in camp were sure something had gone amiss, they'd investigate. Nothing to prevent 'em climbing up that slide notch and finding their quarry had escaped. Be dawn before they could pick up his track. But afoot, he'd be run down in short order.

He needed a horse. And there wasn't but one place to get it. Even if it meant sticking his head right into the Manigault jaws.

Losing no time, Big hunted up his boots and pulled them on, then slung his saddlebags over his shoulder. Feeling his way carefully, he began working around the promontory to its far side, holding to the deep shadows along its base. He kept on going, but with more care yet, as the fan of light that marked the camp grew into sight. When he had a view of the whole camp, he hauled up and settled down on his haunches, sizing it up.

The men were pulled together in a group, talking. Likely speculating that it was damn well time their Indian had accomplished his mission. Or had somehow failed to. Pretty quick they'd be taking steps to verify the situation one way or another.

Searching the shadows to the left of the camp, Big made out a picket line and the shapes of horses. Nobody close by that he could tell. The hundred or so yards between him and the horses were pretty open ground. The studding of shallow rocks and low, scanty brush that laced it might lend him a cover of sorts, but he'd have to crawl the whole distance on his belly to avoid being picked out by the high throw of firelight. In any case, he had no damn choice but to try. . . .

Stretching out flat, he inched slowly out of the deeper shadows, dragging himself along by jackknife twists of his body and hooking his raw fingers into the stony ground. From this position he could no longer tell what the men were doing, but their talk grew louder; he caught a snatch of words now and then. They were becoming plenty excited, some contending they should check things at the rear of the mesa, maybe the Injun had slipped going up and had busted his goddamn neck, others insisting it was time to quit horseshitting around and go straight up the notch, taking a chance the nigger couldn't pick 'em up in the dark.

One man's authoritative voice chopped off the talk with a flat order. Silence. Then the same man yelled, "Lonie! Lonie Bull!"

He paused, waiting for a reply.

The Manigault named Ruel, that likely was. The man

who was giving the orders, according to Lonie Bull. And he was giving some now, breaking the silence with his clear, hard voice.

Big halted and cautiously raised his head enough to take in the scene. Then froze as he was, for one of the men was tramping this way. Seemed agitated by something. His head was down and he was muttering, "Damn damn damn!" in a savage tone.

He passed Big by less than four yards and tramped on to the picket line. He halted there, wheeled around, and came striding back. He was uncomfortably close to where Big lay when he turned again and paced back once more to the horses. He did the same a third time.

The performance made Big's blood curdle. Lord God A'mighty! All this silly-ass bastard had in mind, it looked like, was walking up and down between Big and his goal: the picket line. Goddamn, time was wasting. He couldn't just sprawl here belly-flat till he was found.

As he sure-hell would be, in another minute. Ruel's orders had already dispersed some of the men. Three of 'em remained by the fires with Ruel. Two others were circling around toward the rear of the mesa. Another pair were climbing up the slide toward the notch. In no damned time they would know from Lonie Bull what had happened. 'Less this Ruel Manigault had mush for brains, he'd be quick to order a search around the whole vicinity of the camp, particularly toward the horse line.

And you're trapped smack on your belly where you are, Buford. You go back or for'ard or sideways now, this walking son-of-a-bitch going to spot you sure.

Teeth bared, sweat crawling down his face, Big squinted at the man who was striding up and down. Huh . . . that was curious. It seemed every time he swung face-on to the firelight that there was something familiar in the bastard's look. Big stared harder. Then he was sure. Hell, that face was so like the dead Leon's, he couldn't be mistaken. Yessir, this bastard was a Manigault. He'd be the one Lonie'd said had cold feet about the business of coon-tracking.

Son-of-a-bitch was swinging nearer Big's position every time he turned on this end. Like to spot you any time, Buford, just he looks this way. Christ. Shoot him and they be all over your black ass in five seconds flat. Big fumbled for the bone handle of his Bowie knife, wincing as he closed a bloody raw hand over it. Should he take the gamble? Make a dash out of hiding, cut that Eldon boy's throat, and run for the horses?

It wouldn't do, Big was aware, even as he eased the knife out of its sheath. Directly he was on his feet, all that fireshine 'ud make a clear target of him. Being picked up that quick, not allowed the precious time he'd counted on gaining as he slithered to the picket line and quietly commandeered a mount, he wouldn't stand a chance in hell. Be shot down like a crippled coyote before he got halfway to the horses.

The despairing thought collided abruptly with another, one that sent a surge of hope through him.

Before, he'd abandoned a notion of using Lonic Bull as a hostage to get him past the Lionclaw guns. Ruel Manigault, it seemed clear, wouldn't hesitate to sacrifice any man of his outfit in order to fetch Big. *But would he sacrifice his brother?*

No time to think about it any longer. Nor any need to.

Again Eldon was swinging back this way. As he made his next turn not nine feet away, Big sprang to his feet and took three bounding strides that brought him to Eldon's back. Before he could even take alarm, Big's left arm

95

whipped around his neck, Big's right hand laying the Bowie's keen blade to his throat.

In the same instant, Big yanked Eldon around with him so they were facing the camp, Eldon's body shielding him. "Right here I am, Mr. Manigault!" he boomed. "So's your brother. Look goddamn hard!"

He pushed forward as he spoke, holding Eldon almost up on his toes ahead of him. All eyes turned on them. A man swore. Two others made movements that Ruel Manigault cut off with a motion of his hand. He tramped a few yards toward Big and Eldon, then stopped.

"It won't work, fuzzhead," he said tonelessly. "You're dead already. No matter what you do or try, you're dead."

"But not right yet, I reckon. Not right yet, or so's your little brother. One flick o' this thing and he gonna pour blood like a hog at sticking time."

Eldon made an effort to speak, but Big's massive arm tightened, jamming the words back in his throat. "Listen, man, I got nothing to lose. You stand to lose a brother. Ain't you lost enough kin?"

"On your account, yes," Ruel said softly. "There'll be a reckoning for that, and you'll pay it. If not here, then somewhere. Sometime."

"Sure," Big said. "That's fine. But not here 'n' now, huh?"

"What do you want?"

"My mare's up on that hunk o' rock. I want her fetched down here straightaway. That notch ain't so filled with rock she can't be fetched down."

"Anything else?"

"Sure. One o' your animals and a sack o' grub tied on it. Cask o' water too. We gonna need plenty water. Got a

96

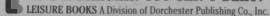

GET YOUR 4 FREE BOOKS NOW—
A VALUE BETWEEN $16 AND $20

Mail the Free Book Certificate Today!

FREE BOOKS CERTIFICATE!

YES! I want to subscribe to the Leisure Western Book Club. Please send my 4 FREE BOOKS. Then, each month, I'll receive the four newest Leisure Western Selections to preview FREE for 10 days. If I decide to keep them, I will pay the Special Members Only discounted price of just $3.36 each, a total of $13.44. This saves me between $3 and $6 off the bookstore price. There are no shipping, handling or other charges. There is no minimum number of books I must buy and I may cancel the program at any time. In any case, the 4 FREE BOOKS are mine to keep—at a value of between $17 and $20! Offer valid only in the USA.

Name_____

Address_____

City_____ State_____

Zip_____ Phone_____

Biggest Savings Offer!

For those of you who would like to pay us in advance by check or credit card—we've got an even bigger savings in mind. Interested? Check here. ☐

If under 18, parent or guardian must sign.
Terms, prices and conditions subject to change. Subscription subject to acceptance. Leisure Books reserves the right to reject any order or cancel any subscription.

GET FOUR BOOKS TOTALLY
FREE—A VALUE BETWEEN
$16 AND $20

PLEASE RUSH
MY FOUR FREE
BOOKS TO ME
RIGHT AWAY!

Leisure Western Book Club
P.O. Box 6613
Edison, NJ 08818-6613

AFFIX
STAMP
HERE

long ride ahead, me'n your brother. You better saddle up his horse too.''

"No!" Ruel's voice turned steel-hard. "Are you crazy? Do you think I'll let you take him away from here?"

"Mr. Manigault, you don't got a goddamn speck o' choice. I tell you what, now. I don't harm your brother long's you don't come after us. I take him with me far's the first ranch or settlement I run onto. Then I turn him loose. He is safe enough—just so long's you don't make after us."

"You've got to be crazy, you black bastard! You think after what happened to another brother at your hands, I'd trust you to a bargain like that? Hell, you'll slit his throat directly you're away from here!"

Big held his voice steady. "Listen, you know how that Leon boy died; you know it was a pure accident. I figured to throw the scare of his life into him, that was all. Sure didn't count on what happened, and I'm sorry for it. I give you my word I don't hurt this 'un. That ain't enough for you, man, you can cut your guns loose any time. But then you got another dead brother. You make up your mind, now."

There was a long silence, broken only by the crackle of flames. Ruel's stocky form was outlined against the fires. His face was in shadow, but his hands slowly opened and closed.

"Your choice," Big said gently. "Sure-dead. Or take a chance on my word. Which it gonna be?"

"Did you kill Lonie Bull?"

"He tied up is all."

"Chase—" Ruel glanced at a crewman standing nearby. "Go call the fellows on the height. Tell 'em to get back down here and bring his horse."

"Saddle and bedroll too," said Big.

The man trotted over to the slide and bawled something up at the men above. Big's whole body was wet with tension, and the arm hooked around Eldon's neck was starting to ache. "You best get that packhorse readied too. And this Eldon boy's nag. Hurry it up, mister. My arm's getting tired."

"Bridge, Chuck, do as he says." Ruel's voice was taut with a hushed rage. "Humor him. It's the last order he'll ever give to white men."

Big showed his teeth in a grin as the two crewmen passed him, heading for the picket line. She-yit, Buford, you going to make it, he thought exultantly. Had been riding pins and needles for a minute there. A hard-as-hell customer, this Ruel Manigault; could never be rightly sure what a man like him might do. But it seemed blood was still thicker than water.

The men who had gone back of the mesa were returning. They were Perce and Ira Denbow. Ruel called to them as they came in sight, warning them not to get rambunctious. Chase was yelling the same message to the men on top as they began climbing down the rocky barricade that partly closed the notch: Jared Denbow; the liberated Lonie Bull; and a tall, gaunt man. They were bringing Tarbaby along, she balking like hell at the descent. Finally they got her to plunge down the steep rubble; it clattered loosely away under her driving feet. She looked all right as they led her over by the fires, no sign of a limp, as Big had feared. And she was restless and mettlesome again; she twisted her head his way and whickered.

Ruel barely glanced at Lonie Bull as the men came tramping up. The Apache would catch hell later, Big supposed, but maybe he was used to swallowing white-man crap. Lonie's face showed nothing at all; it was pretty much the same with the others, though the Denbows wore their feelings plain enough. Be a story none of 'em was like to pass along to their grandchildren—of how a lone darkie had bluffed his way out of their hands.

Big studied the tall, gaunt fellow who had quietly moved up almost by Ruel's side. That big old Sharps rifle held in the crook of his arm said that he was Vrest Gorman, the sharpshooter. Fishy-looking bastard with eyes like chilled marbles. From his look, Big judged that he'd as soon shoot right through Eldon as not, let Ruel give the word.

"Mr. Manigault, I don't want none o' your men moving around the sides o' me. Could be bad for your brother. You tell 'em to shuck all their guns on the ground. You do the same. Then you tell 'em to get all together. Over by the biggest fire yonder where I can see the lot of 'em."

"Do it." Ruel didn't take his eyes off Big. "Do as he says."

Muttering, they discarded their weapons and pulled around the fire in a straggly group, save for the two who were readying Eldon's mount and the packhorse. They'd just finished diamond hitching a pack containing grub and a water keg into place.

"Tell 'em to fetch them three animals over here and get back by the others," said Big.

Ruel snapped the order.

Big eased the Bowie knife away from Eldon's neck, then let go of him fast and dropped his hand to Luis Ayala's old Colt rammed in the waistband of his pants. He brought it up and shoved the muzzle against Eldon's spine.

"Get moving, boy. Up on that horse."

Eldon stumbled ahead of him, rubbing his throat. He reached his horse and leaned a hand on the saddle leather, steadying himself against the animal's flank. He looked at Big with a pale-eyed fury.

Deliberately, Big cocked the pistol. "Get up there, boy," he said quietly. "I don't hanker to kill nobody. But I'll kill you sure as sunrise if you don't do like I say."

Eldon swung up to the saddle. Keeping his face toward Ruel, Big mounted Tarbaby with care, holding his gun on-cock. "Ride ahead o' me now, slow. Mr. Manigault, you wait till we're good 'n' gone before any o' you make a move."

"Nobody will. Don't get nervous." Ruel's tone was drawn fine as wire. "When we meet again you're going to die hard. That in any case. But do him harm and you'll do more; you'll die screaming. I promise it."

Big nodded. "We meet again, somebody's gonna die. I reckon that's so."

Chapter Eight

Dawn. They had traveled through the long, cool hours of darkness and into the gray hours before sunup. Having bought himself a little time now, Big didn't want to set a killing pace. Had him a supply of grub and plenty of water, enough water for a couple days if he shared it with the Manigault. Most important, he had Tarbaby back. Damned good thing, after all, that he hadn't had to leave her in Lonie Bull's hands. Apache had no feeling about horseflesh except for eating it.

Apaches. There was something to think on at this particular time and place.

Even if word had been spread across the territory to get him, he stood a good chance of making the border with a whole hide because whites were shunning a wide stretch of country clear to Mexico right now. At least not traveling it. They were sticking close to the ranches and roadhouses and mining camps. Churupati and his Mescaleros were up

from the Sierra Madres again. Last week they had hit the
Mexican town of Las Truchas below the border; a few days
later they had wiped out a train of ore wagons just above
it, killing the teamsters and running off their mules. That
Churupati's boys were cutting a bloody swath up this way
had made a good reason to plan the last miles of his journey
through a region that was tight-assed skittery about the
Mescaleros.

The likelihood of an actual encounter with the renegades
wasn't great, and just now he'd a sight rather take his
chances with Apaches. Not that the color of his hide would
win him any points with 'em. Most red men who knew
about blacks didn't have much use for 'em. Thought of 'em
as slaves of, hence inferior to, the whites. Injuns set a heap
of store by that kind of measure. At least, though, the
Apaches wouldn't be looking for him—while the whites,
supposing word had gone ahead, would have their eyes and
guns cocked for him in particular.

The sun's red eye was flaring above the black saw-edge
of the Santa Catalinas to the east. Be another day on the
hot lid of hell. What Big planned was to keep moving till
the sun was fairly high, then lay up through the heat of day
till nightfall. It was good, open country for miles, which
meant they could travel steadily by night, with a little help
from the moon. That would conserve the horses as well as
themselves, but the animals would need water soon. Tomahawk Springs lay a ways south of here, and they ought to
raise it around midmorning. Mineralized water that it would
gag a man to swallow, but would do the animals for now.
And there'd be better water at Jackson Tanks, which they
should reach sometime tomorrow.

They would make today's camp at the Springs.

The sun had quarter-arced across the whitish-blue sky

when they came to the place. A wide seep that filtered up through clean sand from an underground source, it stayed wet the year around. The alkaline crust that surrounded it was sun-baked so hard it bore the horses' weights without a dent as they halted close to the water. Close by, chunks of splintered sandstone threw a warm shade.

The Manigault was slumped in his saddle, barely holding onto the pommel. His face was a dirty mask streaked by tracks of sweat; his eyes were red-rimmed and unfocused. He was in miserable shape, suffering from heat and exhaustion, and his hide must have been lily white before the desert sun had got at it. Big shook his head disgustedly. Some fish you have hooked, Buford. Swinging to the ground, he threw his reins, then tramped over to Eldon and took hold of his arm. Christ. He looked and felt as stiff as a board.

"Come on, boy, get you down. Rest your hocks a spell. You ain't no use to me petreefied."

Wordlessly Eldon dismounted, his movements disjointed and jerky. His legs would have given way if not for Big's supporting hand. Big walked him over to a boulder and eased him down in its shadow. Afterward Big let the horses drink, threw off the saddles and pack, and hobbled the animals in a shady niche among the rocks. His palms still quivered raw from the skin being scraped off; they wanted tending.

Numb with weariness, he squatted on his heels by the pack, opened it, and dug out a side of bacon. He sawed off a hunk with his Bowie and then, gritting his teeth, rubbed the fatty meat between his mangled palms. The bit of salt on his raw flesh was excruciating. A body wanted pure-rendered lard for this kind of treatment, but bacon fat was better'n nothing. Anyhow, he hoped so.

Twice, despite the pain of his hands, Big nodded off, his chin sagging to his chest. Both times he jerked his head up, fighting to stay awake. Lord God A'mighty, he couldn't remember being this purely bone-tired in his life. His thoughts were slushy and befuddled, his movements slow as molasses. Hell of a dangerous state for a man in his position who hankered to stay alive.

Forcing his mind to a sluggish concentration, he chewed some more on a worry that had occupied him since last night. He couldn't be sure how well his warning to Ruel had taken. Bastard might have concluded the best way of keeping his brother alive was not to let Big out of his sight too long. He had only Big's word that Eldon would be released unharmed. In this country a man's word, once given, was considered better than a written bond. But that was generally one white man to another. Some might allow a black man equal trust, but Ruel Manigault? Big's lip curled. More'n likely Big Brother would figure any Nigra to do Eldon in, directly he was certain he'd shaken all pursuit. . . .

As Big tenderly wrapped pieces of cloth around his greased hands, his cracked lips shaped an ironic grin. You sure know how the white folks think, Buford, you do for a fact. You so sure you'd think any goddamn different in his place? Maybe you would act different, and maybe that's something. But you don't know. How was it ol' Mose the preacher use to put it in those long-ago sermons when he was a tad? Yeh: *The thought is father to the deed*.

Sure as hell. That's what got you into this goddamn fix, Buford, ain't it?

A man could see a long way across this flat, rock-studded country, with its thin cover of ocotillo and catclaw and prickly pear. Dragging his eyes to focus against the stunning heat, Big kept squinting back across the distance he and the Manigault had come. Only movement out there was flecks of white light dancing off the flats. If the Lionclaw men did give chase, they wouldn't catch up for a goodly spell, even with Lonie Bull coonhounding for 'em. Couldn't have picked up his trail before it was light enough to make out sign. Meantime, he and the Manigault had traveled all night and well into the morning. Gave him as much as four-five hours to catch some of the rest his brain and body were crying for. A risk, all right. Be dead to the world for hours, once he stretched out for sleep. Take an earthquake to budge him. But a helluva sight less risk than trying to stay awake any longer.

Getting the catch rope from Eldon's saddle, Big trudged over to the Manigault, who lay curled on his side. He was too beat out to do anything but mumble and groan as Big trussed him up, hand and foot. Then, stretching out in the shade nearby, Big was asleep almost as soon as his back touched the warm sand. . . .

He woke with a start, his whole body crawling with spidery sweat. Blinding sunlight hit his eyes; he had to blink them clear. Midafternoon. Scrambling quickly to his feet, he studied the flats to the north. No sign yet. If they were coming, they'd come; meantime, he was ravenously hungry. Eldon was half asleep, moaning and twitching. Big removed his bonds. Then Big gathered mesquite brush and built a fire. He gradually fed small sticks into the blaze in order to keep it compact and near smokeless.

As Big was laying strips of bacon in a frypan, Eldon sat up slowly and painfully. "Water," he croaked. His throat was so parched and bruised, he could hardly force out the word.

Big gave a nod at a canteen on the ground, then shifted around on his heels so he could watch all the Manigault's moves. Eldon staggered to his feet and hobbled over to the canteen. He gripped it in both trembling hands as he drank, working the water slowly around in his mouth. He stared at Big, his eyes glazed and puffy-lidded. Finally he said:

"Can I ask who you are? Where you're from?"

"Just a drifter man from 'most anywhere. Your brother Leon now, he figured I was a good old-fashioned darkie. That is how he called me, first we met."

"I guess that was his mistake," Eldon said bitterly.

"Uh-uh, boy. That wasn't his mistake. His mistake was killing an unarmed man in cold blood."

"The sheepherder?" Eldon nodded slowly. "I thought that might have been it. That the Denbow boys lied."

Big spat across his arm. "Figure that all by yourself?"

"I know the Denbows. Knew my brother better still. The sheepherder I never—"

"He had a name. Luis Ayala."

Eldon shrugged tiredly. "I don't know all of what happened, but it's understandable you'd stand by your own kind—"

"What's my kind, mister?"

"Well, a man of color, I mean. He was a Mexican, wasn't he?"

"He was a Basque. He was white as you."

"I didn't know that. I—"

"What you figured, a man only takes up for his kind." Big felt a hot surge of anger. "You right, boy. He *was* my kind, Luis Ayala was. As much as you ain't. And color don't have a goddamn thing to do with it."

Eldon scrubbed a hand over his jaw, scowling. "Maybe I do understand."

"She-yit."

"I'd like to know what really happened. All of it."

"Sure you would," Big jeered coldly. "Lonie Bull told me 'bout you. The tender-hearted one."

Eldon smiled wryly. "Convicted without a trial, am I?"

"So was I. How's it feel?"

"Listen. It can't cost you anything to tell me your side of it, uh—"

"Big Torrey," Big growled.

"What I mean, Torrey, you don't have to trust me to believe you. Or not believe you and then lie about it to gain your confidence. You're not obliged to take a single chance with me. I accept that."

"Well, Jee-*zus*, boy. There ain't a helluva lot else you can do!"

"Right. That's what I'm telling you."

Big stared at him wonderingly, then dropped his gaze to the bacon sizzling in the frypan. Supposing this Eldon boy was in earnest, what could he do to sway his brother's course? From what Lonie Bull had said, not a goddamn thing. Still, by God. Be good if someone knew the full story that Buford Torrey might never live to tell another. If a man hadn't a goddamn thing to leave in this world but his good name, didn't he deserve a better epitaph than a lie that said he'd been shot for a murdering nigger?

All right then. What the hell.

While he forked the bacon onto two plates and dug out some cold biscuits to go with it, Big told how Luis Ayala and the Manigault brother had met their ends. Even made a stab at explaining his own feelings, but then cut himself off. She-yit. Wasn't no explaining to a fellow like this why someone like him would do as he'd done. The Manigault might go through the motions of sympathy, but he was the

107

kind 'ud do the same for a kicked dog. Sort of a reflex. He didn't even have to like the dog. Yessir, this Eldon boy was a gentleman; Big knew the breed from other days. Always dealt kindly with their darkies.

"I believe you," Eldon said, "for whatever it means."

"And that ain't a goddamn thing."

"I suppose not. I've no voice with my brother. He'll do whatever suits him."

"Then you might's well shut up about it." Big handed him a plate of food. "Best chance I got of coming out o' this alive is seeing you stay that way. Here, get some grub in you, keep up your strength. That's the only goddamn good you can do me."

As they ate, Big kept watching across the north flats. And suddenly he sighted the rise of dust he'd expected to finally see, yet had hoped against hope he wouldn't.

He picked up the riders through his field glasses. Yessir, he'd figured Ruel Manigault's mind just right. Best way to ensure Eldon's safety was to keep right on the Nigra's tail, let him know he wasn't pulling any wool over Manigault eyes. Knowing he watched, by God, the Nigra would think twice before doing Eldon harm. That's what Ruel would tell himself. Fact is, Buford, he just ain't gonna give up on you. That's the big truth of it all.

Big let out a quiet chuckle. "Your brother coming, boy. But I don't figure he come much closer."

"Damn him," Eldon muttered. "Does he *want* to get me killed?"

"No-o, I don't reckon. He figure long as he keeps his distance, you be safe enough. Figure I ain't such a damn fool to kill you just because he followed us. Well, he crowding his luck some, but he is right."

Taking no chances, Big chose a likely place in the rocks

where he could lay up with his rifle. But just as he'd expected, the riders hauled up about two thousand yards away, offsaddled, and began to set up a camp.

Watching them, Big felt a savage wave of irritation. This touch-and-go pursuit could continue till they all dropped in their tracks. Except it wasn't likely to happen, simply because all that this Lionclaw crowd had to do was patiently stalk him, holding a distance behind him until, once more, he was too heavy-eyed to fight off sleep. And that would be long before he raised the line with Mexico.

Yep, Buford, that's about it. You don't find a way to shake these sons-of-bitches soon, you be a dead man.

He mulled it over for a time. There was one thing he could try to do. Hell of a dangerous thing. Might stand a chance in a hundred of bringing it off. But he was just desperate enough to make the attempt.

Big waited through the remaining hours of daylight, keeping an eye on the enemy camp. Would have to be full dark before he could do anything. And the same darkness would lend his pursuers cover for anything they might try, such as sending Lonie Bull to sneak up on him again. So Big would have to move away from Tomahawk Springs soon as night fell. Likely they'd expect him to. He just hoped they wouldn't anticipate what else he had in mind.

The sun tipped downward, the last light fading to a hushed purple. As soon as he was sure it was dark enough to hide his movements, Big readied the horses and broke camp. Again he and the Manigault started south. But they didn't go far. Maybe a quarter mile. Then Big halted, dismounted, and ordered Eldon to do the same.

"What is this?" Eldon demanded. "What are you up to?"

"Shut up and do like you're told. I ain't going to ask again. Then lay down on your face."

His voice had a raw edge. Eldon stepped wearily down and stretched out on the ground. Big lashed his hands together and then his feet, yanking them up behind his wrists and securing his ankles to his bound hands. "Don't you go running off now, boy. I be back directly."

So far Eldon had accepted the entire situation with a kind of wry and bitter resignation. But his temper was starting to show cracks. "Where the hell are you going?" he burst out as Big tramped away. "My God, you can't leave me like this!"

Big worked north through the rock field, holding to open places wherever possible so that he could move quickly and easily. When he saw the ruddy glow of fires in the camp, he went ahead more cautiously, creeping low through the brush and taking advantage of the rock cover. Even if he could manage to bring this off, it was going to be a helluva ticklish business. All he had going for him was the element of surprise. And after last night, the men might be a sight more prepared for the unexpected. Still, if Old Man Luck was in his pocket tonight, it wouldn't have occurred to 'em *what* to expect. . . .

Big could have moved quieter on sock feet, but he decided against taking off his boots. Whether he was successful or not, he'd have to clear out of here damned fast. He was near enough to make out the forms of men around the fires, but where the hell were the horses? Had to be on one side of the camp or the other. Out of the firelight. Ought to make things easier, but first he had to locate them.

Big made a slow circle of the camp, steadily working in nearer. The cover here was pretty scanty, but the men by the fires wouldn't be able to pick much out of the surrounding dark. Pretty soon, as he skirted around the northwest edge of the camp, Big picked up small shufflings made by the horses. Now he could just make them out in the faintly reaching firelight. Sure enough—they had the animals on a picket line again. It was stretched between a couple of uptilted slabs of rock.

Big snaked low-bent through the rocks and brush, hugging the ground shadows as well as he could. The men's talk, he hoped, would help cover any small noises he made. He wasn't three yards from a slab that anchored one end of the picket rope when a soft sound made him freeze. Something had darkly moved in the lee of a rock.

Big shrank down on his haunches, heart pounding. Goddlemighty! A man posted to guard the horses—and he'd damned near walked into his arms.

Actually, the guard was a good fifty feet away, but he was straightening up now, shifting away from the rock. A rifle was cradled on his arm. He yawned, stretched, and slowly turned in Big's direction. Frozen to the spot, Big tensed for discovery. He was ready to shoot, then cut and run.

The horses began to stir restively. The guard hesitated, listening. A coyote's cry split the night. The man grunted, then turned away from Big at right angles and walked off into the brush a few yards.

Why the hell had he done that? Big suspected a trick; his muscles coiled with tension. Then he realized that the man was urinating. It sounded, from the violence of his stream and his groan of relief, like a long, healthy pee. Take your time, brother, Big thought.

In the same moment he was catfooting in a fast crouch to the end of the picket line, his Bowie knife in hand. A quick slash parted the rope.

111

Big straightened up, cupping his hands to his mouth. He let go a perfect imitation of a cougar's blood-chilling shriek. Pandemonium rushed over the horse line. Already spooky from desert travel, some of the animals kicked and reared, momentarily entangling themselves in the severed line. Big palmed up Ayala's old Colt and fired three shots above their heads. The panicked horses began to bolt, slipping free, then thundering away into the night.

Big was already in full retreat, plunging through the rock field at a heedless run. The camp was thrown into confusion. Men's voices lifted in angry shouts and curses; several guns spoke. Looking back, he saw spews of gunflame as they surged this way, firing. But firing blind. He kept running in a wide circle and then cut back at an easy ground-eating lope to where he'd left Eldon and the horses.

Quickly untying the Manigault, he urged him into the saddle. In moments they were pushing steadily north through the moon-misted dark. Big felt a surge of elation. He hadn't expected it to be so easy. In one stroke he'd gained a precious lead of hours on his pursuers, depending on how long it took them to round up their lost horses. Some of the animals might only mill loosely about in the dark and be picked up easily, but others would run for miles. And more'n likely, some would never be found.

Yep—might be a day or more before they got back on his trail. Big gave a shout of laughter, his mirth rolling rich and deep across the night.

"What's so damned funny?" Eldon said angrily. "What did you do back there?"

"Why, I just burned me a bridge, that's all—"

Chapter Nine

The next morning Big again made camp and tied Eldon up, then caught a few hours of sleep. Big could have used a heap more of it, but not being sure just how much time he'd gained on the Lionclaw men, he decided not to stretch any rest stop beyond his need. The horses were holding up well and so was his prisoner, though two nights of being relentlessly pushed and proded had steadily eroded Eldon Manigault's halfway sympathy for Big, replacing it with a stark hatred. That was fine with Big; the more this soft boy got his dander up, the better chance he would have of lasting out the trek. They might be trailing a long ways yet; he wasn't forsaking a hole card long as it continued to work for him.

Travel in this part of the territory was always circumscribed by the need for water. Only a man who knew the region as well as Big did would tackle it off the beaten trails and not wind up a dead fool for his pains. He worried some, though, about what he would find at Jackson Tanks. These were catch basins for runoff at the edge of the lava beds, and no saying for a certainty whether they'd be wet at this time of year. He couldn't recall ever before crossing this country at high June. The heat was unbelievably fierce, reflecting nakedly off the parched landscape, pounding against a man's hide through his clothing.

Sweating and sun-punished, Big and Eldon had consumed most of their water by the time they raised Jackson Tanks around midafternoon. The Tanks were set in a rugged formation of bluish-black rock. The water level was lower than Big remembered ever seeing it, but at least it wasn't scum-covered. Climbing to the edge of a basin across basalt rock that was worn and polished smooth as glass, he stretched out on his belly and tasted the water. Warm but clean, better than the rancid liquid in their keg and canteens. He scooped up a hatful of water and poured it over his head. Then he led the horses one by one to drink.

Eldon sprawled flat on his back in some rock-flung shade, an arm covering his face. He seemed incapable of movement or talk. Big left him that way while he built a small fire and prepared a meal. At the same time he surveyed the terrain all around, mostly to eastward, where the fold and ridges of contorted lava cut off his view and might conceal almost anything. He was particularly alert because he knew Jackson Tanks had been an Indian stopover since time out of mind. Once, camping here, he had kicked up a weathered arrowhead in the soil and after a few minutes' search had found several more. Tracks of lion and coyote and antelope showed all around the waterholes: a place to find game as well as water.

Yep, Churupati's boys sure-hell wouldn't miss Jackson Tanks if their swing out of Mexico brought 'em anywhere close to here. Well, no need for the Manigault and him to lay over at this place. Soon as they'd eaten and rested a little, they could load up on this good water and be on their way.

Eldon pulled himself to a sitting position. He looked like plain hell, and he husked out his first words in hours. "How much farther you planning to drag me?"

"Up to your brother," Big said indifferently. "Said I'd drop you off first place with folks we come to. But I ain't looking for folks, you understand. Not long's ol' Ruel keeps hanging on my ass, I ain't. Like I say—up to him."

"So you take it out on me—"

"She-yit, boy, I got no brief for you one way or t'other. You got caught in the middle, and it is a crying shame. But you might's well make the best of it."

Eldon's long, sensitive face hardened along the jaw. "You've lugged me as far as you're going to. I can't take any more."

Big grinned at him. "You got no say in the matter, man. I'll lug you hog-tied across your saddle if need be. 'Low you'll find it a sight easier riding on that sore butt o' yourn. Get some grub in you, you feel better."

"Go to hell. I won't eat. You can't make me."

Big laughed.

His boiled face twisted painfully with rage, Eldon floundered to his knees, then to his feet, and started in a zigzag trot toward the rifle that Big had leaned against a rock. Big swung up off his haunches and took three easy strides, reaching the gun first. He picked it up and turned as Eldon rushed him. Big's arm jerked up, the heel of his thick palm butting Eldon's shoulder. The lightest of punches, it jarred Eldon to a stop and dumped him heavily on his rear.

Eldon's eyes rounded; tears of frustration twinkled at their corners. "You lousy stinking coon!"

"You say what you like—" Big's tone held summer-soft, as his rifle tipped till Eldon was gazing straight up the barrel. "But don't you mouth me like that again. Of late I have been crowded and crapped on by white men till I am sick at my guts with it. I give oath before God you mouth me like that again, I will bust you in more pieces than your brother will want to look for."

He meant it, and Eldon saw that he did. Rolling onto his side, Eldon buried his head in his arms. Big tramped back to the fire, filled a plate with food, and set it on the ground beside him. "You got no say whether you stay alive or you don't. That's up to me. You eat that grub, all of it, or I'll force it down your face."

A horse made a thin, whickering sound. And it hadn't come from one of their animals.

Slowly Big straightened up, sweeping the dark tumble of rocks with his eyes. Nothing. Yet that horse was damned close. If a stray or wild one coming to drink, why had it made no other sound? Straining his ears against the baking silence, all Big could pick up was a droning of flies.

Somebody was with that horse. Somebody who'd arrived at the Tanks ahead of them or just now, but either way had detected their presence and had faded into the field of cramped boulders. Not the act of any company a man'd call friendly. And maybe more than one of whoever. But not many. Or they wouldn't waste time being furtive.

Big had no wish for a fight. He was willing to leave in peace and hoped the unseen party would feel the same. Curtly, he told Eldon to dump on the ground the grub he'd cooked and then to ready the packhorse without delay, while Big kept a watch. The Manigault had heard the horse too; he didn't need urging. He was scrambling to his feet when a rifle shot sent crackling echoes across the lava field.

One of their horses screamed. Big wheeled around to see the packhorse folding down on his knees. Then he rolled on his side, dead.

Eldon yelled frantically at Big, "Give me a gun!"

But Big's attention was all for the two Apaches. They came bounding into sight around the flank of a basalt slab over a hundred feet away. Both had pistols; both began to fire on the run. He swung to meet their charge, shooting as fast as he could lever the Winchester, snugged against his hip.

One of the Apaches crumpled in midrun and went down. Big missed the other, who had already covered half the distance to him. Suddenly the warrior halted and swung his revolver eye-level to take careful aim.

Big fired simultaneously with the Apache. The bullet flung the man around in a spinning fall, kicking and howling.

An arrow sang from somewhere in the rocks. It passed so close to Big that he felt rather than heard its feathered whir. A miss. Or the Manigault might have been its target, for Eldon let out a screech and then toppled to the ground. He thrashed wildly, grabbing at the shaft waving from his thigh.

Big shifted quickly to get out of the open, slipping deep among the rocks where, for the moment anyway, he was on equal terms with an enemy he couldn't see.

Maybe better than equal, if the other had no gun—or what seemed more likely, preferred the bow. Matter of coup pride. Or else the son-of-a-bitch was no shucks with a gun; some red men weren't. Well, this black man knew his rifle like a third hand, but this was no place for using it, close quarters in a jungle of massed boulders. Shifting the Winchester to his left hand, he pulled Ayala's old gun from his belt.

Big crouched, waiting in a tight pocket of rock, scanning as well as he could to every side. Not daring to raise himself too far, he couldn't make out much.

The bastard could be anywhere around him, moving shadow-still from place to place; he was being patient and wary in the true Apache way. His two companions, thinking they'd faced easy odds or taking young men's fever for a risk, had died quickly for it. The brave who'd stayed in hiding was of different stuff. He had the true Apache contempt for an unnecessary risk, even a calculated one. Never give the enemy a break.

Wait him out. Let him make the mistake.

Big could draw on stores of patience too, the deep, sure patience of a man who had hunted wild mustangs. No matter how squirrelly your insides got, you waited. You made your move only when all signs pointed to the right moment.

Reflected by tilted rock surfaces, the heat poured against Big with a blasting fury. Still, he waited unmoving, except for the flick of his eye muscles. A few yards away a big chuckwalla lizard slithered sideways out of a crevice between rocks and began scratching at the earth, kicking up a small fog of dust.

Suddenly it turned its head, as if listening, then scurried back into the crevice and swelled its body immovably into place.

Big listened with a straining intentness. Eldon was giving out sounds of pain loud enough to break a less patient man's attention. But Big isolated another sound for a split second: A moccasin had scraped on rock. He made a guess at its direction and distance from him.

118

Abruptly the Apache came ghosting around a massive boulder just five yards away. Sunlight blazed off the knife in his fist. He sprang, blade arcing high to strike. Big fired. Dust flew from the Apache's shirt; the slug turned him in midleap as Big stepped swiftly aside.

The warrior landed on his side and tried to twist up and around. Big fired again. The brave sank on his back, his blood pouring harshly bright on the earth. He twitched a few times and was still.

Big shuddered and let his fisted gun fall to his side. Lord God A'mighty. Was that all of 'em? He hoped to God it was. Felt like his gorge was about to come up on him.

He swung toward Eldon, snarling, "Get up!"

The Manigault didn't reply. He'd passed clean out from the pain. Big tramped over to him and knelt down to examine the wound. Arrow had sunk a couple inches into the big muscle of the thigh. Poisoned arrow? Could be. Apaches had a trick where they imprisoned rattlesnakes in cages woven of spring willow canes and teased them to a fury by jabbing arrows in and out of the cages. Striking again and again at the points, the snakes would coat them with deadly venom.

"She-yit—"

Big cuffed his hat to the back of his head, staring across the scorched distance to the north. This Manigault wasn't going to be sitting any saddle for a goodly while. Gilman was the closest place he knew of with a sawbones. A slow journey of several days, with Eldon tied across his saddle. Time you got him there, you'd be toting a corpse. And how long before those Lionclaw people 'ud be hellfire on his trail again? Ruel Manigault would be on a tearing rampage by the time he did catch up. And he's gonna for sure, Buford, if you don't get hustling.

He could stay ahead of the pursuers now, he was confident. Having Eldon's horse for a spare, he wouldn't have to push Tarbaby hard. Thin out the load from the dead pack-horse, take only what he needed, and divide its weight between the two animals. He still had a lead of hours on the pursuit. Yessir, he could make it clean to Hermosillo now. Trouble was, he'd have to leave Eldon boy to die.

Big got to his feet, closing and unclosing his fist. Goddamnit, Buford, it's his life or yours. You don't owe no Manigault a thing. Nothing much you can do anyways. And chances are it won't do a lick of good. But he didn't know that for sure, and while the man remained alive, so did the rightness of doing your damnedest by him. It was his doing, after all, that Eldon was here.

Which sort of settled things. Big felt a heavy self-disgust, but reckoned that would be so no matter what he'd decided—except it would be a sight worse if he turned his back on his human duty.

Not thinking about it any more, not daring to, he stirred up the fire and fed in mesquite roots and branches till it was a roaring blaze. Then he cut away Eldon's pants leg around the wound till the whole thigh was exposed. The arrow had gone in at an angle so that it was fixed mostly in loose flesh rather than deep in muscle. Pulling it free, there'd be a danger of tearing the shaft loose of the arrowhead, leaving the point embedded in the leg. Could shove the arrow clear through and then cut the head off, but that would spread the poison.

Taking a hard grip on the shaft, Big braced his other palm against Eldon's leg and pulled with all his strength, slow and steady. He felt flesh tear; the quartz head came free in a gout of blood.

Afterward he let the wound bleed clean for a minute.

Damned good thing the Manigault was out cold. In a sweat to finish up before he came to, Big removed one of his spurs and took it to the fire. He thrust the long, blunt rowel into the heart of the coals, using a couple of sticks to hold and turn it till it glowed a dull red. Then he wrapped his hand several times in a wad of cloth and took the spur from the fire.

The sizzle and stink of burned flesh almost gagged him. But he didn't quit till he had literally charred a crater out of the wound, digging it deeper and wider than the infected area could possibly be. Then he threw the spur aside and walked off a ways and vomited.

When he had made the Manigault as comfortable as he could, Big examined the three dead Apaches. The first two he had shot were young men, the third one in his middle years. It didn't surprise him, any more than did their full regalia for the war trail. Faces painted with broad bars of blue and vermilion. Bodies stripped to the essentials of head kerchiefs, breechcloths, and high, tough moccasins that reached clear to the hips when unfolded to their upper length. Searching a short distance back in the lava ridges, Big found their ponies, shaggy brutes that shied away at his approach. The parts of a butchered antelope were tied on two of the animals.

The three must have been a party of hunters from the main band. Churupati's for sure. Maybe some piece of business had taken the Mescalero leader wide of the Tanks, but he had sent these fellows to fetch game. And when they didn't return, depending how long his other business took, he was likely to come looking for them. An Apache war party never consisted of many men; to lose three at one swipe was no small thing. Losing three to the guns of one man was also a loss of face, one Churupati couldn't afford—a loss that would cry to be balanced in blood.

"Nothing but trouble in the land o' Canaan," Big muttered.

He'd got lucky because a pair of young bucks had got too confident. Wouldn't be that lucky again. No choice at all, looked like. Hang on here with this Manigault boy, they both be dead presently. Couldn't just leave him, either. Had to drag Eldon along even if it killed him.

Meantime, there was the cold grub waiting, and Big was hungry as hell. He wolfed down his share and Eldon's too. Then he made up a light outfit of gear and grub that he could lash to his saddle. As he worked, a notion stirred in his mind. The more he poked it about, the more he figured it was the likeliest thing he could do.

Eldon was starting to come to, groaning, his face wrenched with pain. Sluggishly he raised his head and peered at the mass of bandage on his leg.

"My God." His voice was thin and hoarse. "What did you do to it?"

"Burned it," Big said. "You gonna have a helluva sore leg awhile. Any luck at all, you get to keep it."

Eldon's head fell back. "Guess I'm no use to you any more," he whispered. "I'm about finished."

"You might be tougher'n you think."

"I need a doctor's care. A place to rest and recover. I'd say we're short on both and a long way from either. Those hostiles—"

"I got 'em, all three."

"You said—" Eldon swallowed. "All *three*?"

"Yeah. But they'll have friends'll be along, or I miss my guess. You right: We gotta get traveling. But mebbe not too far."

122

"Is that some sort of riddle? I'm in no way to think about it."

"You got a brother ain't too far on the back trail. Maybe he catching up already. Maybe we'll find him quick."

"You're taking me to—?" Eldon batted his swollen eyelids. "You're a fool. You have a lead on him now. Use it. Leave me—get out of here while you can."

"You in a peart hurry to die, boy."

"I'm talking cold sense." A weak anger fumed up in his voice. "What will it get you? Nothing. And you'll likely die for it. For nothing!"

Big's mouth stretched; he chuckled. "Really gravels your ass, don't it. Getting yourself obliged to an ol' nigger man."

"No, goddamnit, that's not it! It's just—you're a fool in any color, Torrey."

"Yeah, well, a man's got to die sometime." Big nodded slowly, pondering it. "Me, I know what I got in me; I found who I am. That ain't a bad thing to go out knowing, if it's gotta be. There ain't never too many men can say that."

Eldon's eyes seemed to sink; he looked away.

Through the rest of the day, Big rode steadily north. He led Eldon's horse on a rope, with Eldon tied in the saddle. His wrists were bound to the pommel; a line passed under the horse's barrel secured his feet. Helluva brutal way to make do, but there was no help for it. Meantime, Eldon slid quickly into fever; sometimes he was delirious, sometimes unconscious. And so the hot hours passed.

Darkness was cloaking the desert when Big, catching the red-eyed wink of fires ahead, pulled rein.

He blinked exhaustedly. Must be the Lionclaw camp, but the place was way south of where he had driven off their horses. If they'd again resumed the chase and had already come this far, it was probable that Ruel Manigault hadn't waited till all the animals were rounded up. Might have left some of his men and gone on with as many as they could muster mounts for. This was guessing, of course. Hell, they might have recovered enough animals to mount the whole damned crew.

Either way, it sure-hell would be something if Churupati's boys did follow his track from the Springs and they crossed trails later on with ol' Ruel. Big's mouth quirked grimly. It had occurred to him a good deal earlier that if this happened, it'd solve a whole heap of his troubles in one stroke. 'Course, it wouldn't work out that neatly. Even if Churupati was riled enough to engage a sizable party of whites, it was unlikely the clash would result in a wipe-out of either side. Battles hardly ever went thus; besides, Big wouldn't be that lucky. He'd settle for Ruel and Churupati providing each other with one helluva distraction. . . .

Big pushed boldly through the gathering dark toward the fires, all his senses alert. When he'd ranged about as close to the camp as he dared without risking discovery, he dismounted and freed Eldon from his ropes. After lowering the unconscious Manigault to the ground, he felt for a heartbeat. Found it still going strong and steady. Well, we come to a parting, boy—good thing for you. Sorry I had to handle you so rough. Be a sight sorrier if it turns out the death of you. But I got to play out what your brother dealt me. . . .

Mounting up again, Big pulled his Winchester from the boot and rapid-fired it six times. That would bring the Lionclaw people swarming this way like flies on a horse's butt. In minutes Eldon would be in the hands of his friends, and Big, by that time, would have a good spread of distance between them and him.

He rode southwest, cutting away from the trail he had made from the Springs. His spirits began to perk up. Maybe, by God, he would reach that destination in Mexico after all. Those Lionclaw fellows must be worn to frazzles by now. A head-on with ol' Churupati, if it happened, would leave 'em in a sight worse shape. . . .

Wind combed the desert's night face, bringing a broken threnody of coyote song to his ears. Big found himself starting to hum "Massa's in de Cold, Cold Ground." He broke it off. Then he laughed. But the laughter had a hollow feel to it. He had no real wish of that sort against any man. Not Apaches, not Manigaults.

Chapter Ten

Before sunup Big halted to catch a few winks of sleep. At full dawn he was on his way once more, now crossing country that was increasingly familiar to him. By midday he came to the Haines & Harmer stage road, which ran eastwest from Silver City to Gilman, his old stamping grounds. The road followed a southwesterly crook at this point, and he was glad to take advantage of the easy route it offered. He could follow it a goodly ways and cut away from it, southward again, before he reached Gilman. He'd had a hope that traffic on the road might break up his track, but the hope quickly dimmed. It was clear that travel along here had died to a trickle, the stage runs closed down because of the Apache threat.

Big toyed some with a notion of going to Gilman and laying low there for a spell. He knew the country like he knew his own hand. Still had him a few friends thereabouts too. But he quickly gave up the notion. People like the

Manigaults had too much influence anywhere in the territory; he didn't want to involve old friends in his problem. Best to keep going for Mexico.

A single wagon had been along the road no later than this morning. Noting the slow and wobbling ruts it had cut in the deep dust, Big figured to overtake it almost any time. And he did, at Kemper's Wells around the middle of the afternoon. The Wells lay hard by a 'dobe swing station, which Big saw at a glance had been deserted by the Mexican family that usually tended stock for the Haines & Harmer line. The corrals were empty; the station door was banging open and shut in the wind. It had the creepy feel all deserted places have, and Big didn't linger. He rode over to the broad seep a little distance away, and here a high-wheeled prairie schooner was drawn up in some scant cedar shade.

A woman moved into sight from behind the wagon, rifle in hand. Two kids, a boy and a girl, came up beside her, and the three of them watched Big approach. He touched his hat and said "Howdy" as he reined past them to the water hole.

"Good afternoon," said the woman. She had a quiet, pleasant voice.

He felt their eyes on him as he watered his horses, giving their outfit a bleak study. The battered prairie schooner looked to be on its last wheels: The wagon box had cracked along the side and was sagging askew; the weathered, much-patched topsheet was flapping loose; the ancient harness looked to have been patched in a score of places with wire and rawhide. Four rib-gaunt horses stood hobbled nearby, hipshot and droopy-headed, and a lot of ratty-looking plunder was piled under a cottonwood tree.

"Sir," the woman said.

127

"Yes'm."

"I wonder if you would be so kind as to help us. We're in serious need of assistance."

Big gave her a veiled and cautious glance. "What seems to be the trouble?"

"The wheels of our wagon—they seem to be, well, falling apart. Would you look at them, please?"

Big tramped over to the schooner and sized up the problem in a glance. "Yes'm. Wood is all dried out and starting to crack. You have lost some spokes already. What you got to do is take the wheels off and soak 'em overnight, then give 'em a good greasing."

"Perhaps you would assist us, then?"

Big frowned and took off his dusty hat, batting it against his pants. On his way to safety at last, he couldn't afford any delays. Just the thought gave him a pinch of anxiety. "Ain't you got a man, missus? Strange, you way out in the middle o' country like this, you and these young 'uns, with no man."

"My husband is in the wagon. He fell ill shortly after we departed Silver City, but he insisted that we go on. His condition has worsened, however, and I'm afraid it may be grave. We must get him to Gilman—or turn back to Silver City, whichever is nearer—and to a doctor as soon as possible."

"You ain't over two days' journey from Gilman. That is your best bet."

"Thank you. But even two days may be too late. He's very sick—and our wagon may break down at any time. We do need help, as you can see."

Big gave their ratty outfit another morose study. Emigrants, he thought disgustedly. Poor trash to boot. Never seen a lower-down outfit. Nor a dumber passel of people, striking across country where there's Apaches out and nobody else. Kee-rist.

Somehow, though, the rough judgment wasn't convincing. The woman was mannered and well-spoken, a lady for sure, not some hank-o'-hair hardscrabbler's wife. She was firm-eyed and looked intelligent; her gingham dress was faded and much-patched, but neat and clean. The girl, who was around thirteen, and the boy, who looked to be nine or so, were both scrubbed and neat, both of them eying his great height and heft in the awed way to which he was accustomed. Not trash, after all, these folks, by a long way; but sure-to-plumb ignorant of the country and its conditions.

"Sorry," he said roughly. "I got no time to lend you people a hand."

The woman's mouth tucked at the corners; a faint scorn flicked her tone. "Not even for money?"

"No, ma'am, money ain't the thing. Time is what I need, and that's what you nor nobody else can give me."

"I see. Then we shan't delay you any longer."

Too aware of their eyes on him, Big swung onto Tarbaby and tugged his spare horse into motion, and swung back toward the road. He had gone about a hundred yards along it when he pulled up, swearing quietly. God *damn!* He wheeled and rode back to the Wells. The woman, the girl, and the boy silently watched him dismount, walk over to them, and touch his hat again.

"I want to ask your pardon, ma'am. Buford Torrey ain't never turned his back on a body in need. Not till now. Reckon I'm ashamed of it. Will give you any help I can—"

The decision was made that simply. What the hell else could he do? Couldn't leave three helpless people in straits like this, a desperately sick man on their hands. And all of them a sitting prey for the Mescaleros who, coming north, must have crossed the stage road before their wagon came along, or its recent wheeltracks would have led them in pursuit. The Warfields had missed death by hours. And it might still catch up with them. So here was Buford Torrey humanly obliged once more, at the risk of his own neck.

"I'll get the axles up on blocks, ma'am," he told Jennifer Warfield. "Ought to be able to scare up something around the station that'll serve. Then we'll get them wheels off."

"Can we help in any way?"

"Sure. The young 'uns can lend a hand. How you fixed for grub? I got enough to go around."

She smiled, and it made her pleasantly round face almost pretty. Her dark brown hair was pulled back in a plumtight bun; silvered at the temples, it took a chestnut gloss from the westering sun. Somewhere in her mid-thirties, she was of middle height, with a full, matronly figure and large eyes that were serene and pale gray, like first dusk.

"We have plenty of food, Mr. Torrey, and I know that a working man requires a man-sized supper. I'll get to preparing it. I wonder—would you look at my husband first? He's terribly ill, but complaining particularly of pains in the stomach. I'm not really sure what the trouble is. Perhaps you'd have an idea."

Big walked to the rear of the canvas-topped wagon and peered through the pucker hole. A man was stretched out in the wagon bed, covered to his chin by a quilt. A lighthaired man around forty, he had a gauntly handsome face that was pale and drawn, gleaming with the sweat of pain. His eyes were shiny with fever, but faintly sensible as they rolled toward Big.

"Well, hello, Uncle," he said in a faded southern voice. "How did you get here?"

"Rode a long way," Big said. "Your missus tells me you got pains."

"Did dear Jennifer tell you that? Well, I'd call it gastro-enteritis, Uncle. Loss of appetite, nausea, flux, and abdominal pains. In short, a touch of indigestion. Except that it seems to be killing me."

His weak voice was shaded by a sardonic, weary lack of concern. Mrs. Warfield moved up beside Big. "He's being his usual humorous self, Mr. Torrey," she said quietly. "We're not sure what's wrong with him."

Warfield chuckled. "I'm dying of it, my dear. Isn't that enough? Actually, Uncle, my guess would be cholera. I saw enough of it in the Army. Gut is distended and sore as the devil. A condition nicely aggravated by the water I drank an hour ago. From this damned seep." His whole body tensed against a shudder of pain. He closed his eyes, wincing. "If you have something for that in your bag of tricks, old darkie man, I'll be eternally in your debt—"

Big had noticed that the seep was rimmed by a whitish crust. He tramped over to it and tasted the water, finding it faintly alkaline. Shouldn't do a healthy body ill, but would go down like fire on a sore belly. Jennifer Warfield and her kids had begun to gather sticks for a fire. She glanced up as Big returned from the seep.

"As to the cholera," he said, "I reckon your mister is right. Seen plenty of it myself. Comes from eating bad grub. Or drinking bad water."

She nodded, biting her lip. "But Philip hasn't eaten or drunk anything the rest of us haven't. And isn't it contagious?"

"Well, ain't everybody takes the affliction, ma'am. You

131

might see half the people in a place down with it and the rest spared. Same with infected food or water they all took. But this seep now, it's got alkali, which don't give a body cholera but will surely work worse on a body who's got it."

"If only there was something we could do. Anything that would provide him some relief."

"Didn't pack no quinine along? Peruvian barks?"

"No. We've nothing to bring the fever down."

"Paregoric? Might ease his belly by a sight."

She shook her head. "I'm afraid not. We've had to do without a number of useful items on this journey. A supply of medicines, for one."

"Have plenty grub, you said. If you got any canned to-matoes on hand—"

"Yes, we have."

"Well, you strain the juice off a can of them tomatoes and have him drink that. Meantime, if I'm gonna work on that wagon, we best move him out of it."

After Mrs. Warfield had made a pallet of blankets in some shade, Big carried Philip Warfield over to it. Couldn't weight much ordinarily, for he shouldn't have shed such a deal of tallow in a few days of sickness. He reminded Big of a thoroughbred horse that had never got its expected legs under it. Too overbred for ruggedness, too overtrained to meet everyday rigors of living. There was often a streak of crazy in such creatures, and he couldn't visualize anyone but a crazy man taking his family on this desert crossing while an Apache rising was on. Warfield must have been warned—and hadn't listened. And this busted-down wagon and spavined-up team of horses. Jee-zus!

The two kids must have taken a wide streak of iron from their mother's side, for both were bright and healthy and alert. Otherwise they were as unlike as day and night. Wendy was slim, sunny-haired, and cheerful, though she must be smarting from the sunburn on her pale and fragile skin. She readily pitched in with the chore of helping Big scour the station yard for some sizable blocks of wood. In the meantime she rattled all kinds of questions at him, most of which he was hard put to answer. The boy, Tully, was black-haired and tanned to an Indian darkness. He was stocky as a young mule and about as balky. He lagged along poking at this and that, always keeping a distance from Big and never letting out a peep. He kept glaring at Big as if he expected him to cut all their throats without a moment's notice.

After Big had turned up some right sized blocks and wedged them firmly beneath the wagon's axles, he dug away enough of the solid earth beneath each wheel to permit its easy removal. He clucked his tongue, shaking his head in disgust. The wheels were in sad condition, all right. A plumb miracle they had lasted this far. As he worked, he caught the drift of the elder Warfields' voices. Philip Warfield had fallen into a pettish mood, which Big guessed was habitual with him. Mrs. Warfield's voice, as she tried to placate him, held a weary resignation.

"Please don't say that, Philip. Have I blamed you for anything that's happened?"

"You've been thinking it practically aloud, dear Jenny. Do you take me for a fool? What did you tell that darkie about us in order to secure his aid?"

"Philip, please! I asked Mr. Torrey for help, nothing more."

"*Mr.* Torrey—" His laugh dissolved in a fit of coughing. "Have it your own way, Jen. You always did. Never gave a damn what I thought."

133

"I've tried, Philip. Believe me, I have tried."

"Oh, God, we're going to play the martyred little woman now, are we? Why don't you pray for me, Jen? It should help you feel comfortably superior. And I'd expect you to suggest the comforts of the Good Book in this, my dying hour."

Big wrestled furiously with a wheel, his ears burning. He felt a kind of grimy shame in being witness, even unwillingly, to such a scene. He threw a glance at the two children standing nearby, listening too and pretending they weren't, both of them silent and downcast.

Warfield's voice suddenly gentled. "Ah, now I've made you cry. Don't weep over me, my dear. I'm a superannuated sinner, steeped in past contumacies and resigned to hell. 'It matters not how strait the gate, how charged with punishments the scroll—' " His mood veered like the wind; it turned thickly brooding. "Only it's not true. I'm afraid, Jen. For you and the children. God, what have I brought all of you to? End of the trail. A burned-out hope in a burned-out desert. And nothing but a ragged nigger-man to see you through. If he consents to."

"Don't, Philip. Hush now."

Big took the wheels to the seep and laid them in the shallow water. A night's soaking while the wood absorbed moisture and expanded should put 'em back in solid working order. He carried Warfield back to the wagon and placed him inside. In the meantime, Tully gathered more firewood, while Wendy helped her mother cook a supper of beans, salt pork, stewed tomatoes, and coffee, whose aroma gave Big a gut twist of hunger.

He tramped up to the fire, swiping a bandanna across his face. "Well, ma'am, them wheels should be tightened up good as new come morning. Will carry you to Gilman easy if that sorry old rig of yours holds together that long.''

"I certainly hope so. Sit down, Mr. Torrey, and take supper with us.''

"If it's all the same to you, ma'am, I'll eat apart."

"Nonsense. I've cooked up enough extra for two men. You're as big as two men, and you must be twice as hungry, working in this heat.''

Big thanked her. He'd already tended his horses, so he seated himself on the ground, tailor style, to wait supper. Wendy kept bombarding him with questions about his trapping of horses and his days in Mexico, and what-not, till her mother said: "For mercy's sake, dear, give the poor man a rest. He's had a long day."

"A body learns by asking." He grinned at Wendy and winked. "You keep your eyes open, young'un. That's a good thing."

"If *I* may ask a question," said Mrs. Warfield, "are we keeping you from business of your own that's fairly important? From what you said at first, I fear we are."

"My business ain't all that important, ma'am," Big lied with a smile.

Quite a lady, he thought. Seemed as competent a hand as her husband wasn't, leastways at womanly tasks. If she'd come from the quality background that her mannered talk suggested, it was obvious she'd overcome any built-in handicaps of that upbringing. Would make out wherever she was, this lady would, and never lower herself a jot in the doing.

By the time the food was ready, Big was so famished his hands were shaking as he accepted a plate and a cup of coffee. He forced himself to eat slow and mannerly. Jennifer Warfield plainly didn't care a cowchip or less about the color of a man's hide, but all the same, he felt uncomfortable. Pleasant as she might be, she wasn't his kind in the way that someone like Luis Ayala was.

A last banner of sunset retreated down the long slope of sky; behind it slid a purpling wash of night. Twilight cooled around the cookfire, and its warmth was good. After his fourth cup of coffee, Big found himself relaxing some, even enjoying Wendy's chatter. She had as lively a tongue as his Ressie used to. Lord, how that woman would rattle on betimes. He grinned at the thought.

"Mama, can I take Papa something to eat?" Wendy asked.

"He's not hungry, dear, but he said that the tomato juice helped his stomach pains. You might open another can and strain off the juice. We'll have the tomatoes for breakfast."

"Yes, Mama."

"And bring my Bible from the wagon." She smiled at Big. "We have a Bible-reading every night before bed, Mr. Torrey. I hope the meal was satisfactory. I cannot claim very much for my cooking under these circumstances."

Big painfully tightened his stomach to suppress a belch. "Ma'am, I wish I could say I deserve better than you served me, but then I would have to be an angel. You learn to cook like that in New England?"

"You have an ear for voices. Yes, on a Maine farm, where I grew up. My family moved to Boston after my father went into a mercantile business with his brother. We became rich there, and life became very different. I think, though, that my kitchen training was neglected in some ways."

"How's that, ma'am?"

"Well, I wouldn't have thought of tomato juice as a stomach remedy. When I was a girl, my mother shunned tomatoes as poisonous."

136

"Yes'm, lot o' people think so. But it's an old cowcamp make-do. You take tomato juice on an alkali stomach, the acid in it neutralizes the alkali. I been a trail cook off 'n' on." He wryly thought, but didn't say aloud, that it was a caution how many odd tricks a man picked up because he couldn't go too high. Colored man always had a sure-fire job on a crew when a cook's job was open.

Wendy returned to the fire. She set down an empty cup and handed her mother a small, well-worn Bible. "I gave Papa the tomato juice. He's feeling better, I think. He says he wants to talk with Mr. Big."

"Very well, after the reading. Would you make the choice of chapter, Mr. Torrey? It's a courtesy to a guest— an old custom in my family." Mrs. Warfield smiled then. "However, if you're not a religious man—"

Big scratched his head. "Like to think I am, ma'am. Not in the church way, though. Ain't much of a Bible-reading man—" He poked into his memories of old Mose's long-ago sermons. "Reckon my favorite is about the Queen of Sheba."

Pages rustled as she looked for the place. She read slow and measured, in a fine, quiet voice.

"Draw me, we will run after thee; the king hath brought me into his chambers: We will be glad and rejoice in thee, we will remember thy love more than wine: The upright love thee.

"I am black, but comely, O ye daughters of Jerusalem, as the tents of Kedar, as the curtains of Solomon. . . ."

When the reading was finished, Wendy looked at Big. Her eyes were wide and luminous. "I never heard that before," she said in a hushed voice. "It's beautiful, Mr. Big. What is 'comely'? Does it mean nice to look at?"

"Why," Big said gently, "I reckon it means something

like you said first, sister. Beautiful.'' He got up, stretching his big frame. "I best see what Mr. Warfield wants."

He went over to the wagon some yards away and peered inside. The reach of firelight faintly tinged Philip Warfield's pale face. "Something I can do for you, mister?"

"Hardly, Uncle. I'm a dying man. Got anything in your bag of juju lore for that?"

"Afraid not. You might not be as bad as you think."

"Boy, I appreciate the small relief you've given me. But don't give me any of that old darkie bullshit, all right?"

"Whatever you say, boss."

"Good." Warfield coughed huskily. "Now listen. I doubt if I'll make it even to Gilman. Mrs. Warfield says you seem to have pressing business somewhere. Whatever it is, it'll have to wait. Someone's got to see my family safely through, and there's nobody but you."

"Yes seh, I reckon their lives are worth something."

"You trying to get smart with me, boy?"

"No seh."

"Ah. I see what you meant—" Warfield chuckled. "Don't worry, we've enough money to make it worth your while. I keep forgetting we have to pay you people now."

"Oh, you don't want to forget that, boss."

"Very well. Fifty dollars is a handsome sum, I think. I'll tell my wife to pay you. But you don't see a cent of it till the job's done, understand?"

"Sure thing, boss."

Big moved away from the wagon. Suddenly the fire seemed cheerless and inhospitable. He swung off from the spread of light and strode out in the darkness and halted. He shuddered, closing and unclosing a big fist. Screw you, white man. Screw you and your fifty dollars to hell.

Had to dredge up forbearance when a man was in Warfield's condition. But Jesus. It was hard to do when you knew you could break the son-of-a-bitch in one hand. Yes, he thought then, and that's why you don't need to, Buford. The man is dying. You desert that good woman and her kids, you the same as let her son-of-a-bitch husband drive you off. You free to go any time, but you don't let him drive you off.

He grunted sardonically. All that amounted to, when you came down to it, was a mountain of crap. She-yit, Buford, you knew damn well it 'ud go like this. Tomorrow you can't just slap them wheels on the wagon and then ride away leaving these helpless babes to shift for 'emselves. No sir, you got to stick if it gets you blowed to kingdom come.

Which it just could. The precious hours he would lose in escorting a slow-moving wagon to Gilman might just cost him his life. But what else could he do? There was a chance, after all, that Warfield might be saved if he could be got to a doctor. And if that miserable wagon of theirs should bust down on the road and wasn't nobody to fix it, they'd be plumb helpless. There was still the Apache danger too. No, goddamnit, he couldn't in conscience refuse these people whatever protection he could provide 'em.

He stood in the dark, listening to the noises of a desert night. Goddamn. He'd give a peck of double eagles to know what had happened to those Lionclaw fellows. Where they were now, and what they were up to.

139

Chapter Eleven

Lonie Bull was thinking of Big Torrey, and a grin curled the corners of his wide mouth. That is a tough man, he thought, a very tough man. He has run the asses off these white-eyes. It would be better to be with such a man than against him. Yet I have helped the *pinda-likoye* run him almost to death. Lonie's mouth straightened. He was working for the white-eyes and taking their pay; that was not a good thing to forget. He had no particular feeling about it one way or the other, he thought. The black man was a brave enemy, and a man was free to admire an enemy. Still, he should not forget who he worked for.

I am not fighting him, Lonie Bull thought. He had already decided he would not help fight the black man. But it was not wrong to lead the white-eyes to him. That was not the same thing. If they caught the black man and were strong enough to kill him, that was their business. The odds did not trouble Lonie either. He knew that the white-eyes had a thing they called "fair play," to which he saw no sense. He had seen no sign of it, either, among these white-eyes. But that was like the whites. As often as not they talked two ways, and it was hard to tell which way was straight. Anyway, their money was real, and Lonie Bull was an Apache who had learned the value of money.

A flutter of sound close at hand did not disturb Lonie. It was nothing but an owl. His senses identified it and moved past to a blend of other night noises, some close, some far away, instantly weighing each for what it was without disturbing the flow of his thoughts. From his position in the shadows, he could watch the firelit white-eyes' camp and keep a full attention on the surrounding terrain. Now and then he shifted position, shadow-quiet himself as he moved from spot to spot, making a slow circle of the camp.

All that the task required was patience and alertness, and Lonie had endless reservoirs of both. Ruel Manigault wanted him to keep a lookout in case the Mescaleros returned. Lonie doubted they would, but he knew it was never wise to second-guess a *loco* Apache like Churupati. He might come back, after all. He had inflicted some punishment on the white-eyes, but he had taken some too.

The Mescaleros had hit the camp this morning in the gray hours. The Apaches favored dawn attacks. They didn't like to move about at night, when their medicine was weak. At dawn, when an enemy still slept, and before the sun— *chigo-na-ay*—showed his face, was the time to strike. But Lonie Bull too had been awake at that hour. Seconds before the attack came, he had sensed something amiss; he had aroused the dozing white-eyes who was on guard.

As usual the Apaches had gone after the horses first, hitting that side of the camp where they were picketed. There were only a dozen horses, all that had been recovered yesterday after the black man had run them off. These had been enough to mount all the white-eyes so that they could continue their pursuit of him. But half the animals had been swept away by the Apache raid this morning.

Now, though, the Lionclaw men did not need so many horses. Lonie and the white-eyed guard were pouring gun-fire at the Mescaleros as they swept into the camp. That unexpected resistance had somewhat broken the charge, and then the sleeping white-eyes were roused and coming confusedly out of their blankets. Bridge Harney was killed and two other men wounded. Ruel Manigault had gotten a flesh wound that put his right arm out of commission. Lonie had seen at least two Mescaleros fall too, only to be snatched up by their fellows as they retreated. Maybe others had been wounded too. If not for Lonie Bull's alertness, Ruel and all his men would have been wiped out on the spot.

As it was, the posse had taken a crippling blow. The only able-bodied ones left were Lonie, Vrest Gorman, the three Denbows, and Ruel Manigault himself. Ruel had been so shaken by the turn of events that he had ordered a lay-over at the place so they could tend the wounded, including Ruel's brother, while half bracing themselves for another raid. Lonie didn't know what Ruel's next move would be. Considering the shape they were in, they'd be damn fools to take up the black man's trail again. But Ruel Manigault, usually cold-headed, was no longer thinking clearly where Big Torrey was concerned.

He was crazy to get the black man. And he did not give a damn what the cost might be.

Lonie liked the idea less and less. He felt no rancor, but rather admiration, for how the black man had tricked him three nights ago. He was tough and grave and a hell of a shrewd man on trail. He had let Lonie Bull live when he could have helped himself by killing Ruel's tracker. Though that was a weakness of which Lonie himself wouldn't have been guilty, he sensed it was a kind of strength, too, in this black man who had an unswerving code of his own. It was something else Lonie admired: complete self-reliance.

Lonie had made his own way since he was twelve. That was the year that Pinto's Chiricahua band had been driven to the reservation at San Lazaro by Brown Clothes, General Crook, the year that Lonie's divided blood had begun dividing him from his *Be-don-ko-he* upbringing. His mother, a mulatto who had been the maid of a white officer's wife till she was taken captive by Pinto under circumstances Lonie had never learned, had been killed when Brown Clothes' troops had attacked Pinto's *rancheria*. Her death had pretty well dissolved any ties he felt with the Apaches. Since then he had moved freely in the white man's world, watching and learning.

Having seen the ways of all three races whose blood ran in his veins, he felt nothing for any of them. White or black or red, Lonie thought with a calm cynicism that was dead to bitterness, all were most alike in the very differences of which they were so stupidly proud. Each was contemptuous privately or outwardly of all other peoples; it was just a case of who had the upper hand at any given time. He'd known several full-blood white boys who had been captured and reared by Apaches. It never mattered that the boys, if they survived their early captivity, became warriors as good and loyal as any. The Indians never forgot they were different, and because of it never quite trusted them. Lonie, only half Apache, had felt that edge against himself.

If the Apaches were, nevertheless, relatively accommo-

143

dating toward those of different blood, it was still easier, Lonie had found, to make his way among the whites. Maybe the *pinda-likoye* back East were as confined by damn-fool rules and customs as any Indian tribe, but out here the white man's society was so loosely structured that a different one could swim his own current in a sea of strangers. And that suited Lonie Bull perfectly. It meant freedom to do as he pleased, to work for whom he pleased, and to push on when it suited him.

Now and then, though, he met a man he could respect for the man he was and nothing else. The black man was that kind.

Goddamn. It was no good, killing a man like him.

A tall figure was moving away from the fires, coming toward him. Vrest Gorman, Sharps rifle in hand. He was the only white with eyes good enough to pick Lonie out in the circling darkness. Gorman came straight to him and halted.

"Mr. Manigault says for me to take over the watch." His toneless voice grated like something rusty and unused. "You get some sleep, he says."

Lonie grunted. "What about 'Paches?"

"They don't come by dark. I can pick up anything else comes. Mr. Manigault says you gonna need a sharp eye for tomorrow."

So they were going to chase the black man some more. Well, that was what he was getting double pay for. Lonie walked to the fires, sliding a glance across the two wounded crewmen in their blankets. The dead one, Harney, had been buried this morning. Lonie squatted by a fire and poured himself a cup of coffee. Ruel was sitting on the ground by a fire, his knees drawn up, brooding into the flames. His brother lay beside him, soogans thrown over him against the night chill, sleeping fitfully.

All three of the Denbows were crouched beside the other fire, and Jared Denbow was unwrapping the caked and dirty bandage around his son Perce's arm. He gazed at it and shook his head.

"Iffen this gets any worse," he announced, "we gonna take it off you, boy."

Perce's face was gauntly sallow from pain and fever. His head was down, his eyes dull with suffering; he didn't comment.

"We will get that nigger, son, don't you fret. An eye for an eye. We got to; we will follow him to hell's hottest fire."

"I get my hands on that coon," muttered the hulking Ira, "I will crack his goddamn head."

Jared looked at him. "That is well, but watch your evil tongue. The Lord's hand has fallen unnatural heavy on us, and such blasphemy may be to account."

Crazy talk, Lonie Bull thought. He glanced at Ruel Manigault staring into the fire. Ruel was running a slight fever from his wound. His good arm was locked around his knees, the fingers closing and unclosing with a fury that wasn't aware of itself. Mebbeso this was a posse of crazy men.

The black man had become Ruel's personal demon; he had made them look like fools too often. The pursuit whose outcome had seemed dead certain at the start, all odds against the black man, had been cut to ribbons. Pretty clear too that Big Torrey had been responsible for the Apache raid. Eldon had told how he and the black man were attacked by three Mescaleros at Jackson Tanks. The rest of the band, seeking revenge, must have picked up the black man's trail from there. It had led them to the Lionclaw camp. By now the rage Ruel felt outdid Jared Denbow's.

Eldon moaned and tossed, his mouth falling open. He was a pretty sick white-eyes, being in no good shape to start with, then dragged across half of hell by the black man, now taken by the searing fever of his wound. It couldn't have been much of a wound, but the black man had burned hell out of it, though for good reason, as Lonie knew. He wondered what Ruel would do about Eldon and the other wounded men if he planned to chase the black man. Couldn't drag 'em along.

"Ruel," Eldon whispered. His eyes were slitted barely open between his puffy lids.

"How are you doing, boy?"

"I don't know. I'm afraid I've bought it."

"No," Ruel said. "Tomorrow I'm taking you to Gilman, southwest of here. We're closer to there than any other place. We'll make a couple of horse drags to carry you and Chuck Rodriguez. Chase Maginnis and I aren't injured so badly we can't ride. But we can all use a doctor's attention. There's a greaser sawbones at Gilman I understand is one of the best in the territory. Between us, Chase and I can get you two there all right."

Ruel's voice was curiously gentle. Lonie was sure of what he hadn't been before: The boss Manigault was full of concern for his brother's condition. That, more than his wound, was prompting his bitter decision to quit the pursuit.

"And the others, Gorman and the Denbows and Lonie," Eldon murmured. "They'll continue after Torrey, eh?"

"Yes, they'll go after that bastard. And they'll get him. He's been nothing but lucky so far. His luck is due to run out."

"Lucky—Christ." Closing his eyes, Eldon shook his

head wearily. "I told you how it happened with Leon. You call that lucky for anyone?"

Ruel smiled coldly. "You told me what that nigger says happened."

"My God, Ruel, he could have killed me! Or left me to die. He didn't have to bring me back here."

"No, and he didn't have to lead those damned Apaches onto us."

"Hell—" Eldon's whisper was freighted with disgust. "He had a chance to kill Lonie Bull when it would have done him some good. He didn't. Ruel, my God, it doesn't matter how you add it up. We're in the wrong. *We're wrong*. Don't you understand?"

"And don't you understand, you stupid boy," Ruel said in a soft and savage voice, "that I'm not concerned with the right or wrong of it?"

A long silence broken only by a chunky *plop* as a piece of burning wood crumbled in the fire. Then Eldon's gaze moved painfully to Lonie Bull. "Is that how you feel about it too?"

Lonie sipped his coffee and shrugged. "My job is lead you to black man. I'm do what I'm pay for. I lead you to him. I don't fight him."

Ruel glanced sharply at Lonie, his eyes narrowing. Then he nodded once, slowly. "That's all right. You just lead the others to him. That's all you've got to do—"

Chapter Twelve

During the night Philip Warfield's condition had taken a turn for the worse. He was clean out of his head, babbling, quoting shreds of poetry and other whatnots, as the wagon lurched along. Big figured he wouldn't last out the day, but didn't say as much to Jennifer Warfield. Just kept urging the teams onward with a bleak conviction that they'd never raise Gilman in time to do the man a lick of good. The kids sat by him on the high seat, and even Wendy's chatter was subdued. Mrs. Warfield stayed under the wagon topsheet with her husband, doing what she could for him. Tarbaby and the spare horse followed behind, tied to the wagon tailgate. And Tarbaby was saddled, ready for anything sudden.

The wagon creaked and jolted over the rough grade. Here and there the road had been worked over at one time or another by a scraper, but for the most part it followed the contours of the country, going relatively straight and level across flats, kinking like a sidewinder over the irregular spots. The wagon sounded constant threats to bust apart in a dozen places; it swayed like a drunk squaw every time the wheels caught a bump. Anything but a crawling pace was out of the question.

Against his driving urgency to keep moving, Big made several pauses to rest the horses and give the man in the wagon some relief. Big felt torn two ways. He wanted to be honest with Jennifer Warfield and tell her they might as well stop and make her husband's last hours on earth as easeful as possible. At the same time he had the despairing sense of losing distance to the danger at his back. By now, for all he knew, it might be minutes away, rather than hours.

Well then, he thought fatalistically, ain't much you can lose by stopping. You might's well tell her.

The sun was only midmorning high when the decision came. Big pulled up in the shadowed lee of a limestone formation, set the iron brake lever in its ratchet frame, and climbed stiffly down. His muscles cracked as he stretched and unlimbered, glancing at the kids. "You young 'uns get down if you want."

He walked around to the rear of the wagon. "Miz Warfield—"

Her face appeared in the pucker opening. "Yes?"

He said it as well as he could. Jennifer Warfield listened without saying anything. Her eyes were tired and dark-circled from lack of sleep for looking after her man; her expression did not change. And Big thought, feeling suddenly humbled and foolish, she knew all along.

"I didn't want to admit it," she said wearily. "You're right, of course. It is no good. What shall we do?"

"Take him out o' the wagon. Hot under that sheet, and

it is still cool this side o' that big hunk o' rock. Will be till about noon anyways.''

They spread a thick mattress of quilts and blankets on the ground by the rock wall and laid Philip Warfield on it. He was quiet now, his face colorless. Big felt for a heartbeat and could hardly detect it. He was thinking the end wasn't far off when Warfield's eyes flickered open.

''Ahhh—'' His dim gaze touched his wife's face, then Big's. ''Saralee, how good to see your sweet face again. Pomp, you black son-of-a-bitch, where did you come from?''

He smiled peacefully; his eyes drooped shut.

''Saralee was his sister,'' Mrs. Warfield said quietly. ''Pomp was his body servant when he was young.'' She met Big's eyes. ''I'm sorry.''

''No reason to be, missus.''

Big stood up, stretched himself again, and scanned along the flats to the east where the road ribboned away. They'd come from that way when they came. Only question was: when? He felt the woman's curious look. By now she'd repeatedly seen him studying the backtrail. She was, he supposed, close onto the truth. Her next words more or less confirmed it.

''Mr. Torrey, there is nothing to hold you with us. No obligation surely. Your business is still unfinished, is it not?''

''Like I said, ma'am, it ain't all that important.''

Her mouth turned gently, tiredly up at the corners. ''You have done all that you can, for which I am deeply grateful. But—''

''No'm, there's no more to say on't. Whatever happens, I am seeing you and those young 'uns safe to Gilman. I don't want to hear no more on't.''

* * *

Philip Warfield didn't regain consciousness again. Big had seen cholera victims die in terrible fashion, wracked by convulsions, their skins turning blue and their body heat climbing wildly. But Warfield, in frail health to begin with, didn't reach that stage. His failing heart simply gave out. One minute you could still pick up the fine thread of his pulse; the next, it was gone.

Big toiled for an hour and a half in the midday sun, digging a deep grave and laying the blanket-wrapped body in it, then packing the hole with rocks against scavengers. Mrs. Warfield made a marker of two sticks lashed crosswise, carving her husband's name and dates on it. Southern gentleman, Big thought, whose ancestors likely slept under fancy brick and marble in grassy, tended plots. A strange far place for him to find his last rest. But one place was as good as another to them who rested there, come down to it. . . .

They stood around the grave, heads bowed, while Jennifer Warfield read from her Bible, her low, firm voice not faltering. *"All go unto one place; all are of the dust and all turn to dust again. . . ."* Her husband, not a godly man, would have found nothing unsuitable in the reading.

The children took it in about the ways Big would have expected. The girl quietly weeping. The boy standing like a young ramrod, his face frozen, his feelings screwed down tight and fixed to blow up. It would do to keep an eye on him, Big thought. Strange sort of young 'un; no telling how he was affected till he finally let it off.

Hours of daylight remained, and Big wanted to make use of them. He drove steadily through the long afternoon, the wagon pitching and rolling over miles of ungraded road. Mother and daughter stayed inside the wagon, seeking a kind of mutual seclusion in their grief. Theirs was a straight-out healthy grieving; they would be all right in time. But the boy was worrisome. Surprisingly, he declined Big's offer to ride Tarbaby if he wanted; he stayed at Big's side on the wagon seat. Big made a few stabs at talk, to which Tully didn't respond. The boy looked straight ahead and never said a word. Reckon he needs something a man can say, Big thought. Likely a man should say it, as it's a daddy he's lost. But how you make him listen?

They kept going till early darkness. All were dead tired when Big halted by the bed of a dried-up stream. Willows and cottonwoods along its edge hinted at moisture that could be dug for. Once more he used the shovel, thrusting down through wet gravel to wide out a hole that slowly filled with water. Then he led the horses one by one to drink, afterward hobbling them out on the dry, curling grass along the streambank. In the meantime Jennifer and Wendy built a fire and prepared supper.

The meager fare was eaten in silence; even Big was too dog-tired to dredge up much appetite. Watching pale woodsmoke tendril gently up in the still twilight, he shared the family's sadness. It was an hour for hushed and silent grief, not the kind that was tearing and violent.

Leastways he was thinking so when Tully's pain came suddenly to life. He dumped his plate on the ground and scrambled to his feet, staring wildly at all of them. His face worked uncontrollably. Turning, he plunged off into the willow scrub that grew along the streambank.

"Tully," said his mother. "Tully!"

Big laid his plate aside and got up. "You leave this to me, ma'am."

He followed the boy into the scrub, flailing through it with his head down. He came to a sandy clearing on the bank where Tully lay huddled, an arm thrown over his face. Big laid a hand on his shoulder. The boy jerked his arm down, then flung Big's hand away. Tully got warily to his feet, tense and bristling.

"Go away."

"You finally talking, eh?" Big eased down on his haunches and picked up a handful of sand, sifting it through his fingers. "You might's well talk to me then."

"Not to you!" His voice rose to a shrill, hysterical pitch. "What d'you know, you goddamn nigger!"

Big was on his feet in one motion, grabbing the boy by the shirtfront and hauling him up on his toes, shaking him so hard his head bounced like an apple stuck on a knitting needle. "I'm a man and you're a boy. You don't say that to me. Not to no man, less'n you can make the word stick."

The boy's face seemed to crumple; his weight wilted forward against Big's hold. He began sobbing wildly, and Big let him sink to his knees. Then he hunkered down beside the boy, putting an arm around his shoulders.

"Now you saying it," he said gently. "You loved your pa, didn't you? That's all you want to say. There ain't no better way to do it—".

Jennifer Warfield needed to talk. Big sensed it when, after she had bedded the kids down in the wagon, she joined him by the fire, where he was enjoying a last cup of coffee before hitting his blankets. She sat down on the other side of the fire and gazed into it. The tired grief that marked her face only hinted, he guessed, at the deeps of what she felt. She broke a long silence.

"You may not believe it, Mr. Torrey—I don't doubt he gave you cause not to—but my husband was a good man in his way."

"Yes'm. His kids surely loved him. So did you. I reckon that says it."

"Yes. Not all of it, by any means. There's so much—" Her hand brushed her temple in an aimless gesture. "I was teaching at a finishing school for girls when I met Philip. He was in Boston on business, representing some textile interests of his father's. Our family was of the newly rich— marrying into high places was a matter of burning importance to my sisters and me. Philip came of old and established Virginia gentry. He was handsome, polished, charming—and I was only eighteen. All of it obscured, I'm afraid, the very real differences between us."

"Well," Big said awkwardly, "reckon all a body should have to ask 'emselves is, would they do it over again."

She shook her head. "I don't know. That's the sad part of it. Philip's people lost most of their fortune and property in the war. What was left slipped quickly through Philip's fingers after his father died. My father's financial help enabled us to make another start, but Philip seemed to have no knack for success, no real head for business. Failure, hard times, dissipation, and consumption followed, in that order. My father had grown tired of supporting us even before he lost his own money, in the Panic of '73."

"Reckon that's why you wound up out here."

"Yes, as you see us. Another start. I'm not even sure what Philip had in mind this time. He was a good father. A loyal husband. Perhaps that is enough to remember."

"Allowing two fine kids come of it, some folks might say it's more'n enough."

She smiled faintly. "You have a generous regard of things, Mr. Torrey. Were you married—ever?"

Big told her about Ressie and their babies. He had never talked about them to anybody.

"I might have guessed," she said. "The way you have with the children."

"They're elegant kids. Close to how old mine'd be if they lived."

"I couldn't have handled Tully as well. Your people know how to reach the marrow of life and draw it out. So it seems."

"Sure, you know us black folks, ma'am. We just laughs and sings all the time."

She didn't turn a hair; she laughed quietly. He liked that.

"Maybe," he said, "we're more on the inside of life looking out and you are more on the outside looking in. But that's easy to say. I don't know much for sure."

"Some people, Mr. Torrey, might say that is more than enough—"

After Mrs. Warfield had retired to the wagon, Big sat by the fire awhile longer. He felt vaguely disturbed. It was as though something frozen in his innards for eight years had begun to slowly thaw. It shook him up some, even scared him a little, this growing closeness to a white woman and her kids. You know it ain't gonna do you a lick of good, Buford, he thought grimly. Nor them either. So you just whomp down on that thinking. Be a damned good thing, for more than one reason, if he'd never met up with these Warfields.

They rolled out in the early morning at Big's urging. There were no complaints; by now all three Warfields understood that Big had private reasons for haste. They made good time through the morning hours. When they halted at noon to rest the teams, Big was feeling a glow of hope. The country hereabouts was as familiar to him as the palm of his hand. They should raise Gilman by midafternoon.

And still no sign of those Lionclaw people. Had the Apaches cut their pursuit to pieces? Had they given up? Maybe. Just maybe.

He got the leather grease bucket that hung under the wagon and set to greasing the axles. While Mrs. Warfield dug out some cold grub for a noon snack, the kids hung by his elbow, intensely interested in the work, Wendy chattering away as usual. He could feel the undertug of grief in them, but it was well in hand; they weren't letting it throw them by a mite.

Wendy wanted to know more about his mustanging days. "That sounds like a great life, Mr. Big, catching horses."

"It sure was. Pretty lonesome, but free as the wind."

"Gee, yes. I don't see why you quit."

"Reckon I got tired hearing my own voice. No pretty little gal about to bend a man's ear all day long."

"No, honest, why?"

"Well, honey, I tell you. Some men ain't got much belly for catching and shutting up wild things. I plain sickened of it."

"Was that because you were a slave?"

"Could be." Big clamped the cover on the grease bucket and threw a casual glance eastward, giving the back road one of his frequent scrutinies.

"What are you always looking for?" Tully demanded.

Big grinned. That hint of belligerence in the boy's manner seemed natural to him. At least he was talking now. "Gotta keep my bearings," he explained. "Easy for a body to lose hisself in all this country."

"You're fooling again," Wendy scoffed. "All we have to do is follow the road."

"You musta been eating razor soup, you're so sharp. But you never know for sure about roads, sis. They get blowed over by sandstorms betimes. Keeping your landmarks and such in mind is a good habit to get onto, road or no. You ever get lost anywheres, you wait till it's night. If she's a clear one, the stars'll tell your way.''

"They change around all the time," Tully retorted. "You can't tell by them."

"You don't need but one star to fix your way, boy. That's the North Star, and she is always dead north.'' Big chuckled. "Didn't know that when I was a younker on my first cattle drive. I was on night guard and the other boys told me to call my relief when the North Star set. Well, sir, I rode around that herd all night long and every blamed star moved but that North Star. The boys had 'em a whale of a laugh on me come morning.''

Wendy giggled. Big hung the grease bucket under the wagon and straightened up. His eyes sought the road again.

What he saw made him move quickly over to Tarbaby and get the field glasses from his saddle. The rise of dust along the road was plain enough, and so were the five riders. He couldn't make out—yet—who they were. Yet a sense of premonition sent gooseflesh rippling over him. Well, he'd know in a few minutes. Gave him enough time to choose his own place for the encounter. Force 'em to take him on his own terms.

For that was one thing of which he was already dead certain. If the odds had narrowed even to five, he was through with running. It was time to make his last gamble. To stand and fight.

157

Chapter Thirteen

Big was mounting Tarbaby, as Mrs. Warfield descended from the wagon. "What is it, Mr. Torrey?" she asked. "What's the matter?"

"Nothing that's gotta concern you or your young 'uns. There's some men coming up the road. I reckon they're the ones are after me."

"I supposed there was something—" She let the words die.

"Yes'm. They won't bother you none, don't worry. But there's gonna be lead flying when they catch up with me, and I don't want you or yours in line. I gonna lead 'em off from here. If they ask you anything, just say the truth. You don't know what it's about."

"But—!"

Big was already kneeing Tarbaby away, cutting off Mrs. Warfield's objection. Big started down the road at a steady lope, watching the terrain. He knew of a place a few miles ahead where he could hope to make a stand of sorts. Meeting 'em in the open, he wouldn't have a chance. He might stand up successfully to a couple or even three armed men, but he couldn't deal with all five at once. And supposing that sharpshooter Gorman was in the party, he could pick Big off long before they got close.

If he couldn't come out of this alive, Big thought, he could at least make himself damned hard to kill.

When he had covered nearly a mile, Big pulled rein and took a squint through his glasses. The riders had halted by the Warfield wagon. They would have spotted him about the time he had first seen them; they would have seen him leave the wagon. If they weren't yet sure it was he, they would be after they'd questioned Jennifer Warfield; she was too ignorant of the situation to hedge convincingly on her answers. And then, if this really was the Lionclaw bunch, they would be coming on fast.

In a moment the five men wheeled away from the wagon and poured down the road, dust boiling up around them. Big pushed on fast. Two miles farther, he cut away from the road toward a rise of shattered terrain to the south. It rose out of the desert like a single vast formation, which it must have been ages ago. Now it was a broken and crumbled labyrinth of limestone ridges and towers and massive boulders, pitted by deep holes and crosshatched by narrow defiles. Once, years ago, Big had reconnoitered the area out of curiosity. There were places he could fort up and hold 'em off for as long as his ammunition lasted.

But a temporary standoff wouldn't solve anything; they would get him eventually. He wasn't looking to avoid 'em. What he wanted was to end this goddamn cat-and-mouse dodge once and for all, live or die. Once he and they were up in those rocks, the game would narrow down to a fast and violent conclusion.

Big slowed as he reached the edge of the battered formation. He picked his way slowly up its first treacherous slope, not halting till he had ridden Tarbaby into a deep pocket among the rocks partway up. Dismounting, he broke out boxes of .45-.70 shells and filled his pockets. Then he pulled his Winchester from the boot and, leaving Tarbaby in the sheltered pocket, continued up the slope. He worked toward the highest and roughest section of the foremost ridge, where no horseman could follow. Coming after him afoot, they would have to split apart or else come up at him in a single file between the jumbled rocks and spires. Either way he wouldn't have to face more than one gun at a time. But he must keep on the move, never letting them maneuver him into a stationary position.

When he was nearly to the summit, he sized up a likely vantage point, a flat, projecting ledge from which he could spot the enemy's approach. He crawled onto it and stretched out belly-flat where he could peer over its rim. The ledge lay partly in shadow so that its surface wasn't unbearably hot.

Below, the five horsemen had reached the base of the slope. It was an exposed place, and they lost no time piling off their horses and scrambling up the slope, where large rubble that had rolled from above offered some cover. Then they started climbing, working from rock to rock. Big nosed his rifle barrel over the rim of the ledge, but held his fire. Might pick off one easy enough, but that would stop the others and send them into cover. He didn't want to pin them down; he wanted 'em to come straight up and keep coming. Confronting 'em one by one on the rugged upper ridge, if it worked that way, still seemed his best chance. Might only be handing 'em a knife to cut his throat faster, but so be it.

Lonie Bull was lagging behind the others. Now, having reached a nice large rock, he dropped down behind it. Big grinned tightly. So Lonie was having no part of the fight. And that cut the odds by one. It was about time, Big figured, to cut them by another. The other four were now up in better cover. They wouldn't have to stop coming if he opened fire.

Old Man Denbow was moving boldly in the lead, bent low, his sons close behind him, and Vrest Gorman kept cautiously at their heels. Gorman would have no feeling about this business; it was just a job. He was the logical target, but he was cannily holding back of Perce Denbow as they climbed, using him as a partial shield. Perce was laboring painfully along, his crippled arm supported by a sling and hugged against his waist.

Get Perce out of the way and he could snap a clear shot at Gorman.

Big drew a bead on the white sling. His shot knocked Perce over backward; he sprawled howling in the rocks. Instantly the other three dived for shelter. Big quickly levered and fired again, but his shot at Gorman was too hasty and too late.

Gorman and Old Man Denbow and Ira only paused momentarily. Now they began climbing again, slipping upward among the larger boulders, keeping low and moving fast. Big fired rapidly at glimpses of them, but they had his position now and began returning his fire as they ascended. Having used up the advantage of his ledge, Big faded back off it.

He worked slowly along the higher flank of the ridge, staying out of sight among the rocks. For the moment he couldn't see them, and they couldn't see him. All of 'em were on equal footing if you discounted the three-to-one odds.

The mass of splintered rock close to the summit was laced with a lot of loose rubble that rattled no matter how carefully a body stepped. Big sat down long enough to take off his boots and lay them quietly aside. As he was easing to his feet again, he was startled by a muttered drift of voices. They were damned close. He couldn't catch the words, but guessed they were fixing to split apart. Crouching low, Big listened intently, scanning the sun-blistered lift of rock just ahead and to his left. But there was no sound at all now, and it seemed a safe guess they had removed their boots too. . . .

The rocks were hot as hell under Big's sock feet. He decided to keep moving along. At least he was as much the hunter as they were; he too was forcing the issue. It made a twist of feral relief in him. He'd been the fox for their running too long.

A giant shoulder of limestone loomed ahead. From just beyond it came a soft, crunching noise. A single misstep by an enemy. Big catfooted swiftly forward and flattened his back against the rocky shoulder. Then he waited in the throb of furnacelike heat. Sweat drenched his body, but he made no movement except to carefully sleeve his eyes clear.

He couldn't hear a damned thing. If the enemy was coming this way, he was coming mighty slow.

Then a stealthy whisper of sock foot on rock. Yeh—one man edging around the shoulder, moving with infinite caution. He couldn't be over three yards away.

Big took the chance, whirling out away from the rock to squarely face Jared Denbow. The mountaineer gave a grunt of surprise. He jerked the trigger of his leveled piece. The shot thundered as one with Big's. But Big was moving sideways; the bullet that might have caught him dead center only seared along his side. His own shot smashed Jared Denbow square in the chest and flung him against the shouldering rock. Briefly he hung there like a pinned bug. Then he dropped to his knees and pitched slowly on his face.

"Pa—Pa!"

That was Ira. The voice came from off to the right. And Big could hear Ira scrambling wildly across the rocks, coming this way. Big backed around the shoulder till Jared's body was cut off from his view. He jacked another shell into the chamber, hugging the Winchester to his body to muffle the sound.

With any luck Ira would blunder straight into the trap that had killed his daddy. Big had a cold awareness that the shots would fetch Gorman here too. And he would come carefully and probably from another direction. Big only hoped Ira would get here first. *One at a time.* But where the hell *was* Gorman?

A bullet screamed off the flanking rock inches from his elbow. Then the bellow of Gorman's Sharps. Christ! He's at your back!

Big's glance snapped up and around, but he saw nothing. And he didn't wait for a second shot. Gorman might have spotted him suddenly and shot too fast, but he wasn't likely to miss a second time. Plunging around the corner of rock to get out of range, Big nearly tripped over Jared's body.

As he stepped across it, Ira came charging into sight just yards away. He didn't even pause. There was Big straddling his pa's body, and Ira gave a bawl of rage and bulled straight at him. It happened almost too fast for Big to react.

Ira came powering into him, his rifle raised to smash down at Big's head. Big didn't have time to aim his own weapon; he managed to whip it up two-handed fast enough to block Ira's swing.

The gun barrels clashed together. Then Ira's full weight slammed into him and drove him backward, both men crashing to the ground, Ira on top. He was a huge son-of-a-bitch, not as tall as Big but even heavier, and Big was solidly pinned. Ira's rifle was pressed across Big's at an angle, and his massive weight backed the great power of his arms as he pushed down till Big's own rifle barrel was digging into his throat.

Big heaved wildly, but couldn't dislodge him. Big's grip on his rifle didn't offer the leverage to counter Ira's weight and strength. Ira's rifle was sinking hard against his throat. Straining his neck muscles, Big suddenly let go of the rifle and slugged Ira square in the Adam's apple.

Gagging, Ira let up for an instant. Again Big heaved upward, this time tipping Ira's bulk sideways. A final savage heave threw him off.

Quick as a snake, Big began rolling to his feet, but Ira didn't even attempt to rise. He swung his clubbed rifle up from the ground in a sweeping arc. Its muzzle smashed Big across the forehead. He staggered back and fell on his rear, his head banging against the limestone shoulder.

Oddly, that second blow cleared his head. A salty blur of blood stung his eyes. But through its red haze he clearly saw Ira lurching to his feet, his face distorted, raising his gun again. Big's hand moved about six inches to the handle of Ayala's old Colt. With a weird detachment, as if a puppeteer's string was guiding him, he yanked the pistol from his waistband and thumbed back the hammer as his arm came up. He pulled the trigger as Ira flung the rifle to his shoulder.

The shot jolted Ira back on his heels. He grunted with a kind of belated astonishment, then sat down hard. His hand fumbled up to his shoulder; his bearded face squeezed together in a painful spasm. Again he tried to raise his rifle, but he couldn't manage it with a broken shoulder. He flopped slowly over on his side, passing clean out from the pain.

Bracing a hand on the rock, Big tried to drag himself up. He groaned and sank back. His head was splitting with pain; blood filmed his eyes, and he sleeved at it wildly. No good. His vision was fuzzing away, everything turning to a watery blur. Jesus God—what was it? What'n hell was wrong with his eyes?

A soft crunch of gravel close by. Gorman. He was coming. Slow and careful, because the angle of rock had cut his view of what happened. Big rolled onto his knees and one hand, frantically shaking his head, pawing at his eyes. Christ. His brain was clear enough, the blood wiped away. *Why could he hardly see?* He looked wildly about. Everything was a jumbled blur of darks and lights.

Gorman's steps ceased. He wasn't twenty feet away. Seeing Big's helplessness, he chuckled restily.

Big shook his head, blinking. Was that Gorman standing yonder? Or just a trick of sun and shadow? Christ, he couldn't be sure. Shoot fast, Buford. Maybe you will get him. If you don't, it will be over quick anyways.

As his hand tensed to whip up the pistol, a rifle sounded. But it wasn't Gorman's. The shot had a flat, ringing report, not a Sharps' mellow boom. And the dim shape that was Gorman was spinning off balance. But he didn't fall. Suddenly Big's vision was swimming half clear and he could see Gorman pulling around on his heels, fighting to raise the Sharps.

The old Colt bucked against Big's palm as he fired again and again. The white bloom of powdersmoke swirled away. And then he saw Gorman stretched out on his back, bowed grotesquely across a mound of rubble. He was motionless, head twisted sideways, his jaw hanging open.

"Goddlemighty," Big muttered.

Lonie Bull came tramping up, his rifle pointed downward. He halted and looked at Big. The strength ran out of Big's straining body; he was dizzy as hell, and he slumped back.

"You," he whispered. "You done that."

"I shoot Gorman in arm mebbeso little bit," Lonie said. "It's you got him good, black man."

"Sure—I got him. Reckon you wanted to finish this yourself, Lonie. Must want it damn bad. Well, I ain't no way fit to stop you."

"You goddamn crazy mebbeso," said Lonie Bull. "I watch back there." He motioned vaguely backward. "I see you hurt, I shoot, give you chance."

Big stared at him a long moment. His eyes were starting to fuzz up again. Jesus. What was it with 'em?

"Maybe we both crazy, Lonie. You been hounding me to hell 'n' gone. Now you changed sides. What the hell for?"

Lonie shrugged. "*Enju*," he said.

The cryptic Apache word usually meant almost anything. And that, Big knew, was as much answer as he was ever likely to get out of Lonie Bull.

Chapter Fourteen

Big sat by the fire, carefully cleaning and oiling the old Colt. A gun that had given service like this one deserved the best of care. Besides, it was likely there'd be further need for it directly. A grim thought, dizzy and sick as he felt. He had to sit with his back propped against a rock, and unless he stayed quiet, things got all blurry again.

She-yit. Couldn't have cracked his skull. He'd felt it over carefully. 'Course, that didn't mean too much. Once after a horse had kicked him in the head, he'd been dizzy for a week. But what the hell was it with his eyes? It was worrisome, way the least sort of exertion made his sight go dim.

A pot of warmed-over beans and beef was simmering by the fire; Jennifer Warfield was dishing up plates of it for herself and the kids. "Do you think you might manage a bite to eat, Mr. Torrey?"

"I don't reckon, ma'am; thank you just the same."

Big had made it back to the road with Lonie Bull's help; by then the Warfields' wagon was rolling up and they'd taken over the care of him. Jee-*zus*, he hated being in the case of needing care. But he was weak as a kitten; he couldn't even sit a horse. He could barely manage to walk and was so dizzy after taking a few steps that he had to sit down.

Concluding that the two Denbow brothers weren't so badly shot up they couldn't make out for themselves, he and Lonie had left 'em where they were. Later they might come seeking revenge for their old man, but Big didn't figure so. Neither of 'em had their late pappy's fire; like as not they'd taken as much punishment at Big's hands as either of 'em had belly for.

The only big noise still to be reckoned with was Ruel Manigault.

Lonie had told him that Ruel had gone on to Gilman with his wounded brother and two injured crewmen. And all Big could do was curse his bitter luck. The road to escape was wide open now. A day's leisurely ride would have taken him to the border and across it. But the shape he was in, helpless as a baby, he had no choice other than to let the Warfields take him along to Gilman. Needed a spell of rest and quiet. And could be he needed a doctor.

Hadn't told the Warfields about the danger he'd face in Gilman. Jennifer Warfield would try to intercede in his behalf, she was that kind, and he didn't want to embroil her or hers in his trouble. Wouldn't do a lick of good anyway. As for Lonie Bull, if he'd felt a kind of debt to Big for sparing his life, he appeared to consider it paid in full. Not that he'd said anything one way or the other. Having seen Big safely into the Warfields' hands, he had mounted up and ridden away toward Gilman.

Would he tell Ruel Manigault that the man he wanted to kill was on his way there? Big didn't reckon so. All Lonie had mentioned was he intended to tell Ruel he was quitting Lionclaw.

Even if he'd been fit for it, Big had no hankering for a showdown fight with Ruel Manigault. Could be that a showdown might still be avoided, if he could slip into Gilman without Ruel finding out, then manage to lie low a spell till he was recovered enough to clear out and head for Mexico. Hell, he had a few old friends who, if they were still around, would help him out. And one friend in particular.

When the Warfields had finished eating, they helped Big into the wagon. Then the three of them climbed to the seat, and Mrs. Warfield put the team in motion. Though anxious to reach Gilman, now only a couple of hours away, she drove slowly, mindful of Big's condition. Partly cushioned against the wagon's rocking and jolting by a cocoon of blankets, he fought the waves of dizziness and tried to think of other things.

Wendy poked her head through the front pucker. "You all right, Mr. Big?"

"Good enough, sister. Don't fret none about me."

Those two kids, he thought, those brave, beautiful kids and their fine mother. Somehow they kept getting mixed in his head with Ressie and his dead babies. Big rubbed a hand over his aching head. The memories. All the goddamn memories. He'd thought he had laid them to rest for good. Meeting these Warfields had stung 'em back to life with a vengeance. And it was no damn good, no good at all.

Confused, his mind a dizzy whirl, he felt a creeping drowsiness take him despite the pitching of the wagon.

Welcoming it, he let a gray salve of sleep roll over his brain.

Gilman was a good-sized town for the border country. Though isolated, its sun-baked sprawl of adobe and frame buildings was center for a region of wide-flung mining camps. Freighters brought supplies from Silver City; a stage line made regular twice-a-week runs from there. The Apache threat had temporarily cut off freight wagons and stages, but the town's lazy currents of life didn't seem much affected. Big hadn't seen the place in two years, and it didn't show two buildings' worth of difference, he thought, as he climbed down from the wagon outside of the only hotel, the Gilman House.

"If there is a doctor here," said Jennifer Warfield, "I think you'd do well to see him at once."

"Plenty time for that," Big said. "Feel better, some. Want to see you and the young 'uns get situated proper."

He felt a mite clearer-headed, thanks to the sleep he'd caught. Yet his step was none too steady as he led them into the rickety coolness of the old hotel's lobby. Could use a bath and a bed himself, but knew better'n to think he could get 'em here. Old Tinkerman, the grizzled proprietor, was sitting behind the desk reading a yellowed newspaper. He glanced up as they approached, squinting at Big with the dour lack of recognition that Big had expected. Tinkerman had never had a memory for names or faces.

"We don't let to coloreds," he said testily, and went back to his paper.

"These folks is colored white," Big said, "and I ain't staying. Aim to help 'em move in some o' their possibles if you got a room for 'em."

Tinkerman peered around Big's bulk at the Warfields.

He grunted and got to his feet, pushing the register book across. "Dollar a night. How long y'all staying?"

"I don't know that we are," Jennifer Warfield said coolly, "I can't say that I particularly like—"

"Ma'am, might I speak to you a moment?" Big swung a few yards away from the desk and Jennifer, after a moment's hesitation, joined him. "I thank you for the thought," he said, "but it won't do neither of us a speck o' good. This ain't much of a hostelry, but it's clean and I reckon decent enough. 'Fraid you won't find no other in Gilman."

"But you're hurt. You need a bed and care—"

"No need to worry for me. Got friends hereabouts."

Though Big could print a pretty fair hand, he couldn't write except for his name. It took him a few painstaking seconds, peering over Jennifer's shoulder as she signed the register, to decipher the flat impatient scrawl of "Ruel and Eldon Manigault" entered just above her signature. He'd wanted to be sure the Manigaults were signed in here; it was a small assurance to know where they were sleeping.

After helping carry a part of the Warfields' belongings up to the small room they were assigned, Big told them he'd put up their wagon and team at the livery barn. Then he was going to call on a friend, but he promised to see them tomorrow. It was a promise he doubted he'd keep. Having seen them to safety, be better all around if he didn't see 'em again. Be wise too, with the Manigaults here, to avoid the hotel.

He drove the wagon down to the livery, where he was warmly greeted by the aged owner, Jimmy Alvarez. They were old friends. Big wanted to tend to Tarbaby and the other horses himself, but he could feel the dizziness coming back. Just a little exertion had his vision going misty again.

"Like to leave this wagon and the stuff in it here, Jimmy," he told Alvarez. "Belongs to some people come here with me. A lady and her kids, gringos. Reckon they'll claim it when they're ready, along with their horses. If that's all right with you, I'll pay the bills."

"To you, my friend, and to your friends, is no charge."

"Well, thanks, *amigo*. You know if ol' Santhy Mae Potter is still about?"

"Sure, same old digs. That *puta*, she don't go no place. Where she gonna go?"

"Yeh, that's right. Listen, Jimmy, I gonna sort o' lay low a few days. You don't tell nobody you seen me, all right?"

Alvarez's sun-wrinkled face puckered with curiosity, but he nodded promptly. "Sure. You don't look so good, Big. You need place to sleep; my loft she's yours like always."

Big shook his head. He needed a secluded place and somebody to look after his needs, and Santhy Mae was his best bet. "Thanks just the same, *compadre*." He laid an affectionate hand on the old man's shoulder. "I tell you what's afoot later on. Right now I gotta see Santhy."

Alvarez winked knowingly.

Santhy Mae's place was on a cross street at the end of town. It was far from Madam Dubay's fancy big "boardinghouse" for girls, which Big had never seen the inside of. As the town's only colored "lady" catering to colored, Santhy Mae Potter plied a lonely trade, which suited her fine. Color lines were fast-drawn, and you had to go to the big towns to find a large all-colored house. He remembered Santhy Mae telling him how over at Silver City a black cowpoke had got caught with a white woman and how the outraged citizens had strung the cowpoke up and run the woman out of town. Line didn't extend to white boys and colored bawds, though. Never had for Santhy Mae, that was sure.

Her house was a small, snug adobe that used to belong to an old Mex harnessmaker. Big's head was swimming as he tramped wearily up a gravel path and rapped at the door. He waited, leaning against the doorjamb with his head down. A minute passed. She musta turned a whole night of tricks, he thought, and rapped again.

"All *right*, damnit!" came a sleepy voice. The door opened a crack. "Come back t'night 'bout seven, huh, mister? I—for God's sake!" She threw open the door, blinking against the daylight. "That you for sure, Buford?"

"Ain't no other."

"Well, come in, for crying out loud!" Santhy Mae stepped back, tying the belt of her green silk peignoir. "If you don't look like hell. S'pose you got kicked in the head by some outlaw nag again."

"Not 'xactly. I tell you about it, gal. Just lemme sit down."

The inside of the three-room 'dobe was spotlessly clean and neat as a pin. Big sat at the oilcloth-covered table while she brewed up a pot of coffee. She looked pretty good yet, Santhy did, for all her years at the fleshpots. Had kept herself up well. As ever, a mite on the skinny side. Midnight-velvet skin still smooth and unlined. Seemed the most sinful thing about ol' Santhy had always been how little she showed it.

"That's about it, Santhy. I ain't in no shape to face this white man even was I a mind to, and I ain't in shape to travel neither. Need a place to stay. Just a few days."

"Shoo, so you come crying to my doorstep. Sugar, you the hardest man in the world for seeing hide no hair of less'n you need caring for, you know that?"

173

Big shaped a tired grin. His mind budged back to those times when, after he had lost Ressie and the kids, Santhy Mae would drag him out of the gutter stone-drunk and take him to her house to sleep it off. And later, after that mustang had kicked him in the head, how she had nursed him day and night. Both occasions had cost her a pretty penny in tricks. Been plenty other times when he'd simply been lonesome. If he had a gal anywhere, it was Santhy Mae, and she knew it too. For all that, nothing between them had ever jelled on a too-personal basis and was never likely to.

When the coffee was ready, he drank it black and strong. "I tell you one thing, gal. A nice soft bed would sure shine about now."

"I bet. Well, I tell you something too, sugar. Right now you about the ripest thing ever cut wind this side of a stockyard. You ain't plunking it on my nice clean bed 'fore you taken a bath—"

A good long dunking in Santhy Mae's big copper tub eased away a passel of Big's sores and bruises along with days of grime and sweat. Santhy kept adding hot water to the tub till he was half scalded and groaning for mercy. When he finally hit that big soft bed, the whole world floated away, and he slept dreamlessly. Once he groggily woke to a sound of angry voices, Santhy turning an insistent customer from her door, and then he slept some more.

When he woke again, it was full dark. He sat on the edge of the bed, yawned, and gingerly rubbed his scalp. He winced as he touched the raw spots at front and back where a couple of big lumps had raised, legacy of the fight with Ira. As he stood up, the lamplit room spun a little, then steadied.

"Santhy! Where's my clothes?"

"Washed 'em," she called from the kitchen. "Ain't dry

yet. You find a big old robe in the commode. Put it on and come have supper.''

They ate at the small table. Big stowed away beefsteak, fried spuds, and dried-apple pie till he was near bursting. Then they drank coffee laced with whiskey and talked.

"Buford," said Santhy Mae, "I am fixing to retire out of the business. In 'bout a month. What you think of that?"

"Well, it's sure good to hear, Santhy. Got any plans for after?"

"You bet your bottom I have, Daddy. Got my plans and got my savings I have laid by. Gonna move some place I never been, fair-size city like St. Looey, say. Open me a hat-shop. Buford, I gonna be so damn respectable it'd make your teeth ache.''

Big nodded mellowly. "Sure sounds fine. You oughta stay in the territory, though."

She flicked his wrist with a fingertip, smiling. "You come and see me then?"

"Sure thing."

"You know, I would hope to meet a good man. Marry, settle down, have kids. That sound too crazy?"

"Hell no." Big poured a slug of whiskey in his coffee. "You deserve the best. Here's to you, Santhy."

"Ha ha. Thanks." She sounded a mite edgy all at once. "You oughta see Doc Fugentes 'bout that head o' yours, Buford."

"Yeh. Maybe tomorrow."

Santhy Mae got out the makings, expertly built a cigarette, and lighted it, squinting at him through the smoke. "What you got in mind after this jackpot simmers down? Back to seeing after them white folks of yours?"

"They're good people, Santhy."

She shrugged, inspecting a fleck of tobacco on her

175

thumb. "Can't rightly 'spect an ol' sugarmammy like me to know 'bout white ladyfolk."

Big frowned. "Leave it be, Santhy."

"Leave what be? Do I detect a raw nerve there, Buford?"

His jaw tightened. "I said leave it be."

"Why—" Her eyes glinted mockingly. "You ain't gone mushy in the head over a *white lady*, have you, sugar?"

Big leaned across the table, bracing his hand on its edge. "That's enough, Santhy. Just shut up now."

"Shoo, Daddy. Just 'member, all cats is alike in the dark—"

The flat of his hand cracked across her mouth. Then he slumped back in his chair, the anger running out of him. He felt empty as a gutted man. Santhy Mae wiped a finger slowly across her lip and gazed at a thread of blood on it. "Plenty men'll do that to a woman, Buford. I never thought you was the kind. I beg your pardon for saying what I did."

"I—" He stopped. "I don't know what to say."

"Maybe I do. I know you pretty well, boy. You always been a blackbird made his way 'thout flying in through the white man's back door. Always admired that, how you managed it. But you can't cross the line, Buford, and you know it. A white woman's the worst trouble there is for any black man. S'pose'n she have a nigger man like you, she just be sure death for you."

"I know it. No need you belaboring the goddamn point."

"All right." Her face closed; she snubbed out the cigarette in a saucer and stood up. "I just say one more thing. After your Ressie died, and your kids, I looked for a chance with you. I'd a done anything for you. A big ugly bastard like you. Hell, I still would."

"Santhy, you done plenty enough."

"Oh, shut you mouth. I give up hoping a long time ago, Buford Torrey. I'm going to bed. You can join me or you can sit here and drink yourself out of it." She tapped the bottle of whiskey with a well-groomed nail. "Pret' full yet. You can drown a whole lake of tears in that."

When she had gone to the bedroom, Big hefted the bottle gently in his fist as if weighing it. He thought of the memories he had hated, the treacherous memories that used to fashion Ressie into the most beautiful, the most desirable of women, a woman beyond compare, till the pain had grown unbearable. Of how he had hated even more when pain had begun to dull and slip away, leaving nothing at all. Till finally he'd pulled himself up as a man and scourged himself into tasting life again, feeling again, living once more. Now came the Warfields, then Santhy Mae, to open the old scars till they were raw and bleeding. *Ressie Ressie Ressie*!

Big poured his cup full of whiskey and slugged it down, shuddering. Hellfire burned in his guts and slowly ebbed away, fading to a coldness of ashes. He laughed hollowly. Yep, Santhy'd been right. You dreaming again, Buford. Luckily, the dream had died easy this time. Ol' Santhy had laughed it plumb to death.

Chapter Fifteen

"Listen, Buford. I want you to go see the doc. It's early, hardly a soul on the streets. You can be over there and back here inside an hour, you go now. You hear me?"

Santhy Mae had cleared away the breakfast dishes, and the two of them were drinking coffee and smoking the brown-paper cigarettes she had rolled for them. Big grunted a rather surly assent. The dizziness lingered, and his breakfast was quietly churning in his belly.

"All right. Lemme finish my coffee first."

Santhy Mae patted a delicate yawn, giving him an out-of-sorts stare. She wasn't used to rising at this hour. "Tell me something, honey, will you?"

"I dunno."

"What makes you so damn proud? Just what is it, anyways?"

"Pret' early in the day for biting on nails like that."

"I know, sugar, but you give it a whirl. Pretty please?"

Big cleared his throat irritably. "A body got to be proud of what he is. It's all he'll ever be."

"That's a hell of an answer."

"Yeh, to a hell of a question."

She yawned again, flicking ash from her cigarette. "I knew a white man once—"

"I bet you did."

"Don't be nice to me, sugar. Like I was saying, there was this white man, a real educated fellow. He wanted to talk more'n anything else. You know what he told me? He said, lemme see I can get it right, he said, 'Santhy Mae, among the races of the world, your men stand unique.' Yeh, that was it. Unique. 'Look at the Injuns,' he says, 'they fought us like crazy, made us pay for ever' bloody foot of terr'tory we took from 'em. Now look at your men. Blame ever'one but 'emselves for their state. It is a fact, Santhy Mae, that your people in Africa was first made slaves by other blacks who sold 'em to Ay-rabs and white slavers.' "

"My gran'daddy told me the same. What of it?"

"Well, you listen, now. He goes on, 'Santhy Mae, the blacks you come from was the ser-vile ones. It's in the blood. Do you know, when you was slaves ever' one o' your black rebellions was betrayed by one o' your own for massa's cast off shirt or a pair of his wore-out boots? Ever' single one. What you think of that?' "

Big drew on his cigarette, feeling a deepening annoyance. Still on the peck at him, she was dragging out the black woman's old ploy, rubbing his face in the white man. A ploy they managed half the time without really saying it. Give Santhy that, she was straight-out. More or less.

"I think you making it up, you black bitch."

She dimpled a smile. "Shoo. Whoever heard of a black

179

scarlet lady?'' Her eyes slanted to glints of challenge. ''Anyways, it's true.''

His gutty stir of anger got the better of Big's good sense. ''That's what you think of a black man, huh?''

''Forget it.''

''No. That's what you think of us. Well, it's a goddamn lie, Santhy, and your tongue ought to rot for saying it! We fit in the war after Lincoln give his Second Emanc'pation Proclamation. Had us more casualties'n any white outfit. And guess you ain't heard of the 9th and 10th Cavalry. Them buff'lo soldiers is the *best,* the best goddamn regiments in the whole U.S. Army!''

''Yeh, for fighting white man's wars.'' Her mouth parted in a silent laugh. ''They sure enough good for that.''

Big got to his feet in a cold fury, knocking his chair over. He strode to the door and yanked his hat off the coathook. Santhy Mae watched him uneasily. ''Honey, just take it easy now. I didn't mean—''

Big turned and looked at her, fighting a quiver of rage from his voice. ''You meant enough of it. Body don't come out with talk like that 'less a lot of it was spoiling to be said. I tell you, Santhy. Being I'm such a green-gutted worm, I might's well get stomped in real style.''

She pushed back her chair and stood up, her eyes apprehensive and a little frightened. ''Buford—what you going to do?''

''Why, I gonna give myself up, sugar, that's all. To the law. So's I can stand trial for killing that Manigault boy.''

''No—''

Santhy Mae moved quickly to him and threw her arms around him, pressing her cheek against his chest. ''No, Buford! I didn't mean what I said, I swear! I was mad about—about that white lady and you hitting me. You hurt me, I

180

trying to hurt you. God, Buford, I didn't mean it!''

"Maybe you right about that," Big said in an iron voice. "Maybe you right all around, Santhy. Don't you want to find out?"

"No," she wept. "I said a white woman be the death of you. This here won't be no different! You know damn well they won't care about your side of it. Don't do it, Buford. The white man's law ain't for you!"

"Why, gal, you ain't talking against the white man, are you? He is strong and brave and wise. Ain't that what you been saying?" He reached up and closed his hands around her wrists and pulled her arms away. "Time we find out. I'm sick of it, woman. Sick o' running, sick o' being set on by white men, by you, the whole damn business. That boss Manigault, he says I'm game to be hunted down. Naw, not even that. Just a nigger. Well, they don't try game animals, and mostly they don't try niggers. You-all been wondering just what I am. Time you got showed—''

Big shoved her away, threw open the door, and stalked out. A pounding of blood filled his head; he hardly heard her cry after him. He tramped down the street and turned the corner, and then the full tide of dizziness hit him. He stumbled and fell to his knees, shaking his head.

He looked up. Everything was a shifting blur again. He stayed as he was, biting down on the violence roiling in him, till the world came back to focus. Easy, man. Easy. Don't make it too fast.

Maneuvering back to his feet, Big plodded on slowly, his head down. Jee-zus, he was being a damn fool again. Letting Santhy sting his pride like he was some wet-eared kid!

Of course, that wasn't all of it. Not even a good part. Santhy Mae's words had merely roughed up a sore that had festered in him ever since he'd begun all this damned running. He had nothing to prove to Santhy or the white man or even himself. But he had by God the right to hold up his head as a man and not be driven like a dog. Anyways, how far could he run? If Manigault really wanted him bad enough, he'd finally get him. Manigault money could hire detectives to find him and assassins to gun him. Even if not, he'd spend the rest of his life looking over his shoulder and jumping at every odd noise.

If he was going to stop running anywhere, this was rightly the place. Where else would he stand even a beggar's chance of escaping the hangrope in a trial? Nowhere but here in Redrock County, his old stamping grounds. He was known here; the Manigaults were the strangers. Not much to peg a nigger's hope, but what else did he have?

As Santhy Mae had said, the streets were almost deserted at this hour. The frame courthouse was set kitty-corner to the Gilman House at the town's main intersection. Big tramped onto its porch and paused there, leaning against a gallery post while he fought the dizziness. Then he walked around to a side entrance with the legend SHERIFF painted above the door. Gilman had a town marshal, but the place to dump this business, he figured, was square in the lap of county law.

He beat heavily on the door. Waited. Then hammered on it again.

The door was opened by a paunchy, olive-skinned man in his shirt sleeves, a coffee cup in one hand. He yawned and scratched his balding head, giving Big a heavy-lidded stare. "Don't kick the door down, man. You want som'thing?"

"Wanta see the sheriff."

"I'm the sheriff. Come in."

Big stepped inside and the man closed the door, sipping his coffee as he crossed to the battered rolltop desk and slacked into a swivel chair behind it. He yawned again, motioning at the only other chair in the room. "Sit down. You want som' coffee? She's fresh."

"No thanks." Big remained standing in the center of the room, legs apart, his stance solid and implacable. "Thought ol' Jim Buck was sheriff in Redrock County."

"He retired a couple months back. Got crippled by arthritis and never finished his term. I was his chief deputy. Ramos Apodaca is my name. Yours is—?"

"Torrey, Buford Torrey."

Apodaca's eyes veiled; his half smile faded. "Ah," he said softly.

Big settled gingerly into the chair. "I reckon Mr Manigault been to see you."

"Yes—yes." The sheriff rested his elbows on his chair arms, steepling his fingers. "He has asked me to be alert for any news of a man named Torrey. A big Negro man, he said."

A corner of Big's mouth lifted. "He put it just that way, huh? Well, I saving you the trouble, sheriff. I come to give myself up."

"Why?"

"I want to go on trial. Want to get this whole mess in the open. Tell my side o' the story. You interested in hearing it?"

Apodaca moved his hands vaguely. "Of course. Of course, señor. Please."

Big told everything that had happened from the time he had ridden into Luis Ayala's sheep camp up till his arrival in Gilman. He told it carefully and with all the detail he could remember. When he had finished, the sheriff got up

183

and paced a slow circle of his office, rubbing a hand over his jaw.

"Say you are telling the truth," he said. "You think you will be believed? Against Mr. Manigault's word, I mean?"

Big shrugged. "I'm known hereabouts. Ought to get me a hearing, anyways."

"But you would stand trial up north, in the county where the, ah, killing was committed. I would have to send you there. Haven't you thought about that?"

Big hunched forward in his chair. "There's a thing called change of venue, ain't there, where you can get a trial switched to som'eres else?"

Apodaca moved restlessly; he nodded. "Uh, well, if a judge can be shown there's a reasonable bias against the accused. Of course, you got to prove—"

"Look, sheriff. What I figured, you might hold me here, sort of in protective custody, till the whole thing gets thrashed out." Big paused. "You see, I get sent back to that county the Manigaults run, I don't reckon I gonna leave it alive, ever. They'll see to that."

Getting up, Apodaca walked to the single barred window that faced the street; he stared out. "Mr. Torrey. Ruel Manigault told me his story too. It is not so different from yours. I think he does not give a damn what I think. He wants you, that is all, and he wants you dead. He does not care how he kills you, I think, just so it's done."

"Yeh," Big said dryly. "That's what I think."

"He has many men, this Manigault. Not here, but it won't take long to have them fetched. Or better, he has money, eh? He can hire a bunch of riffraff here. There's plenty such in this place. To get a jail busted into and a nigger lynched, you will pardon my saying of it, he won't have to pay them much. A few dollars and a few drinks will do the job.''

''You got a job too,'' Big murmured. ''How much they pay you to hire deputies to do it?''

Apodaca smiled thinly. ''Señor, I can deputize every man in this damn town if I want. You know what good it will do? A few of my own people will stand for being deputized to save—you. A few and no more. Where does that leave me?''

''Stuck smack in the middle of your stinking job, I reckon.''

A slow rise of blood darkened Apodaca's face. He turned from the window. ''Listen,'' he said in a strained voice, ''you know what it means for a man of my race to hold a public position like this in a county where Anglos have all the power?''

''I can guess.''

''Guess!'' Apodaca laughed harshly. ''That is all you can do. Listen. I pulled myself up from dirt; I taught myself to read and write English. The deputy's job I got long ago because Jim Buck needed a man to handle the Mexican element. Finally, two years ago, I got the chief deputy's job because I was next in line for it and because Jim Buck was a fair man, but *Dios!* he made me earn it. Now. I have the chance, before the next election, to show what a Mexican can do in this job. So I tip my hat politely, I smile a lot; I swallow the sneers and slurs; I bend over backward to be fair—''

''You got to bend forward a ways too,'' Big observed.

''What do you mean?''

''To kiss all them nice white fannies.''

After a moment's silence, Apodaca said tonelessly,

"There's still Mexico for you. That's where you were headed."

Big chuckled quietly.

"Som'thing is funny?"

"Well—" Big got up from his chair and lounged toward the door. "If I told any other nigger I had this much trouble getting put in jail, he'd never believe it."

"I think," Apodaca said softly to his back, "you are a troublemaker. I don't want trouble in this town."

"Yeah, I noticed." Big paused, hand on the doorlatch, and looked at him. "What you do if I make trouble, throw me in jail?"

The jeer deepened the heavy flush in Apodaca's jowly face. "You been warned. Get your horse and ride out. Take your fight with the Manigaults somewhere else. Or I won't be responsible for what happens."

"Responsible is a place you ain't been." Big's voice had gone low and taut and ugly. "I tell you, sheriff. I been running and running, and I'm a tired man. I ain't going to run no more. Not for no Manigaults, not for you. If you won't help me, you stay clear out of my way."

Chapter Sixteen

Jerking the razor along his jawline with short, impatient strokes, Ruel Manigault cut himself. He cursed and kept doggedly whittling away at the rest of his beard. A damned nuisance having the use of only one arm, the left one at that. As simple an act as pulling on his boots was a chore. But he'd have to manage this way a good while yet. The Apache bullet had nicked the bone of his forearm. It wasn't only incapacitated, it was painful as hell. Dr. Fugentes had removed a bone chip from the surface of the wound and had said there might be more, but it would be best to let them work out.

Ruel's mood was black as he toweled away traces of lather and copious blood from his cut jaw. He swore again and dipped the towel in cold water and pressed it over the cut as he prowled slowly, restlessly around the cramped hotel room. Should have been such a damned easy thing, nailing up one nigger's hide. They had begun as a posse of ten able-bodied men, and where were they now? Bridge Harney dead, Chuck Rodriguez and Chase Maginnis put out of action, after an encounter with Mescaleros. Ruel had a crippled arm and Eldon had escaped death by a narrow margin. Vrest Gorman and Jared Denbow were dead, the two Denbow sons were out of it, and Lonie Bull had quit. . . .

When the bleeding was checked, Ruel threw the towel aside and awkwardly got into his shirt, working the right sleeve over the thick bandage on his arm. He adjusted a sling around his neck so it would cradle the arm. Afterward he shrugged into his coat, leaving the right sleeve empty, clamped on his hat, and left his room, locking the door. He stepped across the hallway to the opposite door and knocked.

"Come in," Eldon said.

The room was hazy with smoke. Eldon was sitting up in bed, reading a newspaper and smoking a cigar. Scowling, Ruel moved over to the window and wrestled the warped sash up a few inches. "I'm going over to the restaurant. Want any breakfast sent up?"

"Ham, eggs, fried spuds, and coffee," Eldon said cheerfully. "And ask that red-headed waitress to bring it up, will you? She's heavily solicitous about my health."

"Glad you're feeling so damned bright-eyed and bushy-tailed," Ruel growled. He picked up one of Eldon's cigars from the washstand, bit off the end, and stuck it in his teeth, fumbling impatiently in his coat pocket for a match. "I suppose you slept like a baby, not a care in the world."

Eldon grinned. "Why not, brother mine? *I* haven't lost any niggers."

Ruel snapped a match alight on his thumbnail and

touched it to the cigar. "You damn near lost a leg on his account. Isn't that enough?"

"Oh, hell," Eldon said disgustedly. "Let's not hash that over again. Look, Ruel. The way things have gone, the two of us are lucky to be alive. Why not settle for that? In a few days, if the stages are running again, my leg'll be well enough that we can take one out of here. Let Torrey go. God knows we've done enough to him, and he to us. Let it go, can't you?"

"Not while I know he's alive," Ruel said softly. "Not till I've seen that uppity bastard over a gunsight."

"He's proved himself eminently unkillable, I'd say," Eldon observed dryly. "Quit dreaming. He's got away; he's long gone; can't you get that through your head?"

Ruel walked back to the window and stared down at the street. "We don't know where he is. He might have been hurt in that shootout. Lonie wouldn't say. But I'll find out."

"Oh? And how the hell will you manage that? You don't even know where it happened, for Christ's sake! Only Lonie knows, and he's quit you cold."

Ruel was silent, his jaws set together.

Lonie Bull had come in yesterday afternoon with word of the fates of Gorman and the Denbows. The way Lonie had very simply told it, they had overtaken Big Torrey and he had taken on all four men and disposed of them singlehanded. And what the hell, Ruel had demanded wrathfully, was Lonie doing all the while? Lonie had indifferently replied that he'd stayed out of it, as he'd said he would. Also, he was through working for Ruel and wanted his pay. Ruel had furiously pressed him for details. What had happened to the nigger? Was he hurt? Hadn't Lonie any idea what he'd done next? When Lonie had clammed up, having divulged all he intended to, Ruel had cursed him and said he could go to hell for his pay. Lonie had shrugged again and walked out. . . .

Hard as the fact was to bite on, Eldon was right. No way in hell to find out where Torrey was now unless the Denbow boys showed up in Gilman. Lonie had said that both were wounded; they might come here seeking a doctor. Besides, they were still working for him, weren't they? On the other hand, with their old man dead, they may have decided, as Lonie had, to quit the whole business. Still, they might show up. He could wait a while longer.

"Look," Eldon was saying in a quiet, persuasive way, "Forget about him. We've a ranch to run; you've said so yourself. All you're doing is beating your head against a wall. I've never seen you let anything get under your skin the way—"

"I've told you why we have to get him," Ruel snapped, not looking around.

"Because a passel of landgrabbers will move against Lionclaw now? That may have been your reason to start with, Ruel. It isn't any longer. He's made you look the fool, and you—"

Ruel's whole body jerked; he snatched the cigar from his mouth. He braced a hand against the window frame as his stare focused tightly on the courthouse.

God. Yes. It was him. Torrey. He'd just stepped out of the sheriff's office, big as life. Now he was swinging slowly down the street toward its south end.

Ruel turned from the window, a fierce exultance boiling up in him. He looked at Eldon a moment. And he laughed.

"What the hell?"

"He's here, my boy. Your fuzzhead friend is right smack on that street down there."

He started for the door as Eldon strained himself upright,

yelling, "Ruel! My God, what are you going to—? *Ruel!*"

He kept wildly yelling Ruel's name, over and over, as Ruel spun into the hallway and then plunged down the staircase. He crossed the lobby at a run and hauled up on the porch outside. He swung his eyes against the flat rays of the morning sun. Torrey was moving slowly upstreet, weaving a little. Like a drunk man. Or a hurt one.

Ruel slapped a hand against his hip. Damn! He had left his gun in his room. He started back into the hotel, then halted. He'd never shot a pistol left-handed—and why take a chance? The nigger wasn't unkillable; he'd just been damned lucky.

So far. There was a way of being dead sure.

Hance's Mercantile Store was just across the street, by the courthouse. A gray-headed man was fumbling with the door, unlocking it for the day's business. As Ruel started to cross the street, he thought fleetingly of Rodriguez and Maginnis, the two wounded Lionclaw men who had accompanied Eldon and him to Gilman. They too were installed at the hotel, and Maginnis, at least, wasn't so laid up he couldn't lend a hand now.

But why? He could handle this himself, Ruel thought. He smiled with a wicked relish. It would be easy.

He came up behind the gray-haired man, touching him on the shoulder. As old Hance gave him a startled look, Ruel said: "Open shop in a hurry, will you? I want to buy a shotgun."

As he left the sheriff's office, Big knew with a bleak certainty that he was in no shape to back up his tough speech to Apodaca—a fact that didn't dent his hard core of resolution. But if he was done fleeing from Manigault, he'd still be forced to lie low till he was fit for a showdown.

So it was back to Santhy Mae's for now. Would Apodaca betray his presence here to Ruel? Not likely, Big thought. The sheriff was so anxious to avoid trouble, he'd probably keep silent in the hope that one or both of them might leave Gilman before they tangled by intent or by accident. On his part, Big decided he wouldn't go looking for fireworks, nor back off from them either.

Right now he'd best do as Santhy Mae had urged and visit the sawbones. He tramped slowly upstreet. As he neared the livery stable, old Jimmy Alvarez came hobbling to its archway and raised a hand to flag him down.

"Hey, *amigo*. I thought you was laying low."

"Just come from making some medicine with your sheriff," Big said sourly. "Is Doc Fugentes still got his office at the same place?"

"Sure, up at end of town. What is this trouble you in, Big? Maybe a friend can help."

"I don't reckon, Jimmy." Big briefly explained his situation. "Sheriff might be of help, but he staying set on his big fat star."

"Ha! That *hijo de puta*." Alvarez spat. "You get nothing from him."

"Well, some ways I don't blame the man much. Be a heap o' ruckus to kick up over one busted-chip nigger—"

A movement that crossed the tail of Big's eye made him break off, turning his head sharply. Boy, he thought wryly, you getting too jumpy. Just a man coming out of a store. . . .

Only the man was coming straight this way. And he was toting what appeared to be a long gun of some sort. With a growing tightness in his innards, Big shook his head; he squinted his dim eyes to focus. Then he recognized Ruel Manigault. And he saw the long-barreled shotgun.

Moving away from Alvarez, Big started up the street at

a swift lope, hugging the buildings. He threw a glance over his shoulder. Manigault was coming after him on the run.

Big yanked the Colt from his waistband and braced to a halt, turning on his heel. Now clear of Alvarez, he was ready to meet the man who had dogged him across the damned territory. But the brief exertion had done its work: Even as he brought the pistol up, Ruel's form was a fading blur in his sight. He was barely able to make out that Ruel was pulling to a stop too, raising the shotgun one-handed. His right arm was bandaged, but he had it up, awkwardly bracing the shotgun's twin barrels across it.

That big old Greener would rip him apart like wet paper at this range, Big knew. And no time to get his aim, way his eyes were acting.

He sprang for an alleyway that opened between a saloon and the feed company building, diving into its mouth just as Ruel opened up. The shotgun's roar beat down the sound of double-O buck, exploding shreds of clapboard from the saloon's corner. Plunging through the alley, Big crashed into a trash barrel and fell to his knees. He stumbled back on his feet and out of the alley, then cut away at a loose angle from the buildings.

All he could make out ahead of him was a haze of pale greenery that he knew was a forest of mesquite. If memory served him, it was too thinly scattered to lend him much cover. But he also remembered a certain steep-sided arroyo a ways back. Guided mostly by blind instinct, he pressed into the mesquite at an unsteady run. The greenery opened up before him, and he picked out the shadowy trough of the arroyo.

Big hit the edge of it without stopping and slid down the steep cutbank in a moil of dust. Morning shadow lay cool and long in the patches of tangled brush that laced the

193

gravelly bottom—heavy brush that might have concealed him except that his tracks in the soft ground above would lead plainly to the arroyo's edge. Once Manigault followed him here, he could take his time about beating the arroyo brush for his quarry. As Big recalled it, the narrow wash ran pretty straight for a couple hundred yards. It came off a long ridge at its upper end and finally petered out in an outwash fan about fifty yards below his present position.

He scrambled up along the arroyo to where brush grew thickest. It would hide him from any but a close scrutiny, forcing Manigault to hunt him out. With any luck Ruel would come near enough for him to get a clear shot before Ruel spotted him. Coming to a dense clot of foliage now, Big squirmed his way into it and stretched out on his belly.

From here he could faintly make out the crumbled track of raw earth where he had skidded down the cutbank; Ruel would see it too. Would he be hotheaded enough to come barreling straight into the arroyo and make a nice target of himself? Maybe, Big thought. He's that dead set for your scalp, he was ready to kill you on the street in front of witnesses.

Well, why not? Who of any consequence would care if the cattle baron gunned down the nigger? Not that butt-kissing sheriff. Not any white jury that might sit in judgment later on. If it even got to court. And supposing you get him, Buford? What you gonna tell a court about that?

Wait till it happened. One trouble at a time.

Lying quiet on the cool gravel, Big felt his pulse slowing, his eyes clearing somewhat. He held his bent arm in front of him, elbow braced on the ground, palm sweating around the pistol's grips. Just keep watching. You don't know what he'll do, so watch everything you can see.

Manigault came edging into sight along the rim of the cutbank.

He peered down at the marks of Big's descent, afterward throwing a swift glance up and down the arroyo. Big tried to line the sights of his pistol, but they wavered. He gripped the Colt in both hands and steadied it. Still a far range for a handgun. If he missed and gave away his position, he'd be at Ruel's mercy. Charge of buckshot would rip his brush cover to hell and make a spread that was bound to find him at this distance.

Big waited, his eye still fixed along his gunsights. Get down this way, man. Come on.

Ruel stepped over the bank and plunged down it, digging in his heels. Brush partly screened him from Big's view as he bent over, scanning the arroyo's gravelly floor. Then he began moving slowly in Big's direction, the brim of his hat cutting a slant of shadow across his eyes.

Big squeezed off a shot.

He heard Ruel's hard-driven grunt. But he couldn't have more'n nicked him. Ruel dropped to one knee and threw the shotgun to his shoulder, his right arm bracing it. With a desperate energy, Big heaved himself sideways, scrambling partly free of the brush, as the shot came. The heavy pellets pounded brush and earth so close by that its outer spread flung dirt against his arm.

Frantically Big rolled again, piling out of the brush now and slamming into the cutbank on his left. Simultaneously, he realized, Ruel had flattened himself against the same bank. A slim angle of it now hid each man from the other's view.

For one agonizing moment, Big hesitated. Had Ruel discharged both barrels? Or had he slipped in a fresh load after firing at Big on the street? If not, he couldn't break the shotgun, remove the expended shells, and reload with much speed—not with a bad arm.

It's a chance, boy. Take it. Won't be no other.

Lifting up suddenly, Big stepped out in the clear, quickly covering the dark blur of Ruel's shape. And Ruel was set for him. Down on one knee, his shotgun tipped ready across his right arm. He fired in the same instant Big did.

A massive blow drove Big's leg from under him. He wasn't aware of falling till the earth slammed him in the face. Dazedly, half blind with shock rather than pain, he rolled onto his side. He realized he had lost his gun. He groped wildly for it. Then he heard Ruel's shuffling tread as he moved forward. He heard him speak in a flat, calm voice.

"You're all through, mister. You're finished."

The sliding click of metal on metal told him that Ruel was awkwardly reloading the shotgun.

Then the blaze of pain flooded Big's pulverized thigh. Setting his teeth, he fumbled one hand to his blood-soaked leg and gripped it hard and waited for the first surge of agony to recede. As it did, so did the red throb of his blindness. Ruel's stocky form came into focus. He was standing maybe two yards away, and he'd kicked Big's gun well out of reach. His mouth was like a seam in brown granite; he studied Big with a kind of impersonal patience.

The shots had whipped the landscape to utter stillness. In those fleeting seconds, as his sight cleared and Ruel slowly brought the shotgun up, Big had the sharp taste of life's sweetness as he had never known it.

Eldon Manigault spoke quietly. "Don't, Ruel. Don't."

Big turned his head till he saw Eldon standing on top of the cutbank, a gangling figure clad only in long-handled underwear. His face was white and pinched with pain as he braced himself erect on one good leg and another that would hardly bear his weight. He held a pistol, its hammer drawn back to full cock. And it was pointed at his brother.

Ruel shook his head once, slowly. "You've never had the guts to shoot anything. Even a chicken. Don't fool with that thing, Eldon. It might go off."

"Ruel—put the shotgun down."

"Why you damned, stupid boy—" Ruel's mouth stirred with a heavy contempt. "Don't you know I never stop anything I do till it's done?"

"You're going to stop this thing. I swear you are. You're going to stop it right here."

For answer, Ruel looked back at Big. Deliberately he thumbed one of the shotgun's hammers to cock. And Eldon shot him.

The bullet drove Ruel off-balance against the bank. He sagged down on his knees and stayed that way. One hand was pressed over his ribs, and he gazed dumbly at the blood pouring over it, afterward turning his eyes to his brother.

"Do I have to shoot again?"

Ruel squinted painfully; he opened his mouth and closed it. Then he let the shotgun slip to the ground.

"It's done, Ruel. It ends right here. If you take it to the law, I'll tell any sheriff, any judge, any jury what really happened. If I have to, I'll defend Torrey myself. And you listen—" Eldon's voice twanged like a taut wire. "If you ever go after him again, I'll kill you. I swear to God I'll kill you!"

Chapter Seventeen

It was Jimmy Alvarez and his stablehand who, supporting Big between them, got him up to Dr. Carlos Fugentes' quarters above the assayer's office. The job of maneuvering Big's great bulk up the rickety outside stairs and onto the operating table left the two men exhausted. Dr. Fugentes, a spry, wizened man with a gray, neatly trimmed Vandyke and more energetic cheer than Big had seen in a man his age, broke out a demijohn of wine and almost ceremoniously served whopping drafts of it to Jimmy and the stablehand. Afterward he handed the demijohn to Big.

"Drink all you can, señor. It's going to hurt like hell, digging out those shot."

"Thanks, Doc, but ain't you got ether or something?"

Dr. Fugentes patted his shoulder. "It's better to be drunk, believe me. Go on, drink."

Big kept right on swilling the strong, sour wine while Doc pried out the shot, clinking the pellets into a plate. He

198

was still at it when Tinkerman from the hotel came banging at the door and said there was a white man needed attention.

"Who is he?" Doc asked.

"Mr. Ruel Manigault."

"Again? He will have to wait. I am tending another man. Go away."

Having cleaned out the shot, Fugentes clucked his tongue and shook his head. "*Dios*, that's a real mess. Maybe I can save the leg, but you going to be one sick fellow, I think. You better stay here awhile. I got calls to make, so maybe you know someone will take care of you?"

Big nodded dreamily, his mind drifting. "Yeh. You fetch ol' Santhy Mae Potter, Doc."

"Ah, the *puta*. She is a lady of mercy, maybe?"

Doc had a great sense of humor, but it hurt too much to laugh. "Yeh, you could say that. You fetch her, huh?"

Big was installed on a cot in the doctor's big back room. It was the only sort of hospital that Gilman boasted; just now he was the only patient. Jimmy Alvarez went to enlist Santhy Mae's aid. . . .

A week of bad days and nights went by.

Big's leg swelled to again its normal size, and he was in fever and delirium practically all the time. He had flickery impressions of Santhy Mae constantly at his side, tender-handed as a mother. If his leg needed hot packs on it, there was Santhy Mae to change them. If he tossed and raved, there was Santhy Mae to hold him down. If he burned with fever, there was Santhy putting water to his lips and wiping sweat from his face. They had been through all of it before, but the full meaning of it had never reached him till now.

199

And finally it touched him, sick as he was, with a deep and sure knowledge.

At last the fever broke, and he slept the clock around.

When he woke, he was wasted to weakness, but he was hungry. Santhy Mae wasn't around; Dr. Fugentes answered his call. Santhy had gone to catch some sleep herself, Doc said. And added with a new respect in his tone:

"That is a remarkable woman, my friend."

Big agreed. He told Doc about the couple of fierce wallops on the head he had taken during his fight with Ira Denbow. He described the resulting dizzy spells and blurring of his sight.

Fugentes stroked his Vandyke. "I have looked at the head. It probably is only a mild concussion. Already the injuries are healing. I have seen such things before. They need only time and rest. I think when you are back on your feet, you will find the difficulty has passed."

"Sure hope so."

Doc lighted up a pair of cheroots and handed one to Big. "By the way, there is a family of gringos, the Warfields. They been around asking about you."

"Did they? Nice of 'em." Big drew luxuriously on his cheroot. "Doc, what 'bout Ruel Manigault? He come out of it all right?"

Fugentes nodded wryly. "He is very tough, that one. Not the big bull you are, but he is a very tough man."

"Yeh, don't I know it."

"When you finish the smoke, I heat you some broth. Then you sleep some more. Sleep all you can."

There was a knock at the outer door; Doc went to answer it. Big recognized Jennifer Warfield's voice, and then he heard Doc say, "Not too long, if you please, señora." A moment later the three Warfields entered the room.

"I hope you don't think we're paying a belated call, Mr. Torrey," Mrs. Warfield said. "We've come often, but you haven't been up to visitors."

"Yes, ma'am, Doc told me. I want to thank you."

"How are you feeling now, Mr. Big?" Wendy asked.

"A heap better, sister, thanks."

They chatted awhile, but on Big's part at least, the conversation was awkward, touched by a stiff discomfort. They were damned fine people, these Warfields, but not his kind after all. Had seemed a heap easier being in their company back on the desert. Here in such civilization as Gilman represented, all the differences seemed magnified. He was relieved when Mrs. Warfield said:

"I think we'd better take our leave now and let our friend take his rest."

"Mighty nice o' you to drop by," said Big. "Got any idea what you will do now?"

"We'll be going on to San Francisco. One of my sisters lives there. She and her husband will help us out, I'm sure, till we've made some definite plans. But we couldn't leave here without saying good-by—and thanking you."

"Hello," Santhy Mae said quietly. She stood in the doorway, twirling a bright parasol in her hands, and she looked carefully at the Warfields, then at Big. "Hope I ain't interrupting nothing."

"These folks was just leaving," Big said. "Mrs. Warfield, I would like you to meet Miss Samantha Mae Potter."

Santhy Mae nodded stiffly to Jennifer Warfield's friendly greeting and the pleasure she expressed at meeting one of Mr. Torrey's friends. After the Warfields had left, Santhy pulled up a chair by Big's cot and sort of collapsed into it.

"Whee-oo," she said dryly. "That's a lady right enough.

You said so, and you wasn't whistling 'Dixie,' sugar.''

"Yeh." Big reached out a hand and closed it over hers. "But I reckon ladies come in all shapes 'n' sizes.''

Santhy Mae smiled. "All colors too, Buford?''

"Yeh. All colors. So do men, Santhy.''

"Sure." She looked downward, shaking her head. "I'm sorry for that, Buford, I—''

"That a new dress you got on? It's mighty pretty.''

"You think so?''

"I think something else too. It's pretty enough to get married in.''

She looked at him a long moment, then pulled her hand gently away from his. "You lightheaded, boy. You fooling with me. Don't fool about that, Buford.''

"My head's plenty clear. More'n it's been in a long time. Santhy, you ought to know when a man means it.''

"You—you talking about for good, Buford. That ain't nothing to rush into. Ain't how *I* feel," she went on quickly, half angrily. "It's you, Buford, the kind of man you are. There's a lot—a whole lot of things you'd have to put out of mind. I don't know as you could manage it.''

Big grinned. "Because I'm so damn good?''

"Oh, no." She eyed him sardonically. "You a sure-fire sinner, you are.''

"Yeh, and who ain't?" He captured her hand again. "We'll have plenty time to talk 'bout it. But listen, you don't wait to close up shop, you hear me?''

"It's closed, man. Closed for good." She laughed, a little shakily. "All the same, we don't rush into nothing. You give it time, Buford.''

"Why," he said, "I don't see no problem there. This man won't be rushing nowhere for a good spell, Santhy Mae.''

BONNER'S STALLION
T.V. OLSEN

Winner of the Golden Spur Award

Bonner's life is the kind that makes a man hard, makes him love the high country, and makes him fear nothing but being limited by another man's fenceposts. Suddenly it looks as if his life is going to get even harder. He has already lost his woman. Now he is about to lose his son and his mountain ranch to a rich and powerful enemy—a man who hates to see any living thing breathing free. That is when El Diablo Rojo, the feared and hated rogue stallion, comes back into Bonner's life. He and Bonner have one thing in common...they are survivors.

___4276-2 $4.50 US/$5.50 CAN

BREAK THE YOUNG LAND

T. V. OLSEN

Winner of the Golden Spur Award

Borg Vikstrom and his fellow Norwegian farmers are captivated when they see freedom's beacon shining from the untamed prairies near a Kansas town called Liberty. In order to stake their claim for the American dream they will risk their lives and cross an angry ocean. But in the cattle barons' kingdom, sodbusters seldom get a second chance...before being plowed under. With a power-hungry politico ready to ignite a bloody range-war, it is all the stalwart emigrant can do to keep the peace...and dodge the price that has been tacked on his head.

_4226-6 $4.50 US/$5.50 CAN

T. V. OLSEN

Winner of the Golden Spur Award

THE STALKING MOON

Army scout Sam Vetch is finally ready to settle down and start a new life on that quiet New Mexico ranch he's been saving for all these years. He has no way of knowing that his cherished wife had once been the woman of Salvaje, the notorious Apache chieftain known as The Ghost—and that she has borne two sons by him. When Salvaje comes to claim what is his, the duel begins—a deadly contest between two men of strong will, cast-iron courage, and fatal honor—a duel that can only end in tragedy under the stalking moon.

_4180-4 $4.50 US/$5.50 CAN

ARROW IN THE SUN
T. V. OLSEN

Bestselling Author Of *Red Is The River*

The wagon train has only two survivors, the young soldier Honus Gant and beautiful, willful Cresta Lee. And they both know that the legendary Cheyenne chieftain Spotted Wolf will not rest until he catches them.

Gant is no one's idea of a hero—he is the first to admit that. He made a mistake joining the cavalry, and he's counting the days until he is a civilian and back east where he belongs. He doesn't want to protect Cresta Lee. He doesn't even like her. In fact, he's come to hate her guts.

The trouble is, Cresta is no ordinary girl. Once she was an Indian captive. Once she was Spotted Wolf's wife. Gant knows what will happen to Cresta if the bloodthirsty warrior captures her again, and he can't let that happen—even if it means risking his life to save her.

_3948-6 $4.50 US/$5.50 CAN

Dorchester Publishing Co., Inc.
P.O. Box 6640
Wayne, PA 19087-8640